1

"Now, have you got everything?" Nan asked for what felt like the twentieth time that day, passing me my overnight bag on the doorstep. "Have you got your swimming costume? Toothbrush?"

"*Nan!*" I said, going bright red. I could see the girls looking out of Chloe's mum's car window. "It's only a party. Please stop worrying."

"I do worry," Nan said. "You don't know who's around. Can't trust anyone these days."

"She'll be fine," Grandad yelled from inside the house. "They're sensible girls. Aren't you, Molly?"

I wish Nan wouldn't worry so much. She always calls me her "baby", but I wish she'd treat me more like a grown-up sometimes.

Chloe's mum waved to us out of the car window, phone to her ear and laughing. She looks more like a babysitter than a mum. She's the type of woman I see modelling in my nan's weekly magazines – beautiful and glamorous, with expensive clothes and a posh car. She looked too young to be married to Chloe's dad, who seemed more like my Grandad's age. Even though Chloe spoke about him all the time, no one saw him much.

Nan looked disapprovingly at Chloe's mum, but I rushed to the car as quickly as I could and put my bag in the boot.

I couldn't wait for today. We'd been chatting about it in school all week. I love our girly sleepovers and this one was going to be *epic*, especially as it also happened to be Chloe's birthday.

A lot of people wonder why Chloe and I are friends at all. Nan says we're like chalk and cheese. Chloe is very loud and outgoing and I'm very shy. She's incredibly pretty, with bright golden hair and I'm ... well ... I'm just plain old me. Nan says I'm beautiful, but it's hard feeling beautiful when you're compared to someone like Chloe all the time.

Chloe and I have known each other since we were babies and we're inseparable. Neither of us have any brothers or sisters, so we basically became the siblings we never had. We'd spend every summer holiday together, having picnics in the park and playing Knock Down Ginger. We'd play princesses and dragons and try on her mum's clothes when she wasn't looking. We even wore friendship bracelets for years, until Chloe took hers off recently because it looked too "babyish".

Chloe's parties are always the best because there are never any rules. Last Halloween her parents organised a spooky murder mystery, where Barbie's killer – who'd left her decapitated on the grass outside with tomato ketchup around her neck – had left clues around the house and garden for us to find. It led to a massive midnight feast – full of pizza, sweets, crisps and cake – that we ate and ate and ate until we felt sick. At a few of her sleepovers, we'd been allowed to watch some 15-rated films, until Neada's parents found out and got mad at Chloe's mum for letting us watch them. It caused a huge row and Chloe kept calling Neada a baby for weeks afterwards.

Neada is my second-best friend after Chloe. She's a bit ditzy, but she's always happy and smiling so it's hard not to like her. Her parents are from India and are very protective of her, but not as much as my nan is towards me. They have huge parties, full of dancing, and I can't help but wish I had a big family like that.

Jess came to our school last year. We're becoming better friends over time but, like me, she's a bit quiet so it's been hard for us to get to know each other properly. She's a tomboy and very sporty. She's obsessed with football and her bedroom is covered top to bottom in Manchester United posters.

Chloe told us this birthday would be the best she'd ever had. We were going swimming first – my absolute *favourite* – and then off to her house in the evening for a sleepover and takeaway. We were allowed to go in the pool without any parents watching us and Chloe said there was a good chance some boys would be there.

I've never quite understood the appeal with boys, but Chloe's been interested in them a lot lately. She acts differently when they're around, like over-the-top giggling and being silly. Neada, Jess and I can't help but laugh when she acts like that.

I have one best boy friend (NOT the romantic kind – gross) called Ed, who's in swimming club with me, but he's different to all the others. Ed's funny – not annoying like most of them in my class are – and we've known each other since we were five. He always looks scruffy and never brushes his hair properly. Chloe says he's annoying but I can't help but find everything he does hilarious.

Nan was waving from the doorway as we drove off but I was too embarrassed to wave back, especially in front of Chloe. I don't think the other girls noticed. At least, I hope they didn't.

"Hi, Molly!" Chloe's mum said, looking at me in the mirror. "You look well! Are you excited about going swimming? We all know what a water baby you are."

"Shut up, Mum," Chloe said.

Chloe's mum didn't blink. If I spoke to my nan like that I'd be in so much trouble, but Chloe talks to her mum however she wants and somehow manages to get away with it.

"What are you *wearing*?" Chloe said, turning

5

round and eyeing me up and down. I went scarlet. Nan had dressed me in dungarees with stars across the front, which looked incredibly babyish compared to Jess's jeans and sweatshirt and Neada and Chloe's pretty dresses. I couldn't help but feel annoyed at Nan for making me feel so stupid.

"Look at you girls, growing up so fast!" Chloe's mum said, quickly changing the subject. "I can't believe you're off to secondary school soon!"

Oh. Secondary school. I'd almost forgotten. Or, at least, *tried* putting the thought of it to the back of my mind. Chloe says you need to have a boyfriend by the time you start Year 7, or have at least *kissed* a boy by then, or you'll probably get bullied by the older girls for being frigid.

That, and the idea of new people, new teachers and older boys, scared me silly. I didn't *want* to kiss a boy, let alone call one my boyfriend.

The only thing I was happy about was the fact I had my friends with me. And as much as Chloe could be mean to me sometimes, I felt safe knowing she'd be there by my side.

2

I love swimming. I go to the local pool every Wednesday night with Mr Davidson, my PE teacher, and some other people from our swimming club at school. There's only ten people in our group and we have so much fun.

Mr Davidson says I'm a fantastic swimmer with "great potential", and deep down I know it too. He'd been a professional swimmer when he was younger but decided to become a teacher because he wanted to earn more money. He always says I should come to more swimming classes like the others, but Nan can't drive me there in the mornings because of her rota at work.

I could stay in the pool for hours. I put my goggles on, hold my breath and imagine I'm a beautiful mermaid, swimming at the bottom of the ocean among the sand and coral reefs. I pretend I'm from a regal underwater kingdom, with a beautiful king and queen for a mum and dad, and all the friends and presents I could ever wish for.

Grandad took me to the leisure centre all the time when I was little. He'd taught me to swim without armbands by the age of three. We'd drive there every Saturday and swim all morning, then treat ourselves to sandwiches and crisps in the café after. We'd watch the grown-up swimmers from the café window, diving head first into the water.

"You'll be as good as that someday," he'd say confidently.

Nowadays we can't go swimming together because Grandad isn't feeling too well. He'd been a gymnast when he was younger and had always kept himself fit, but now his hip hurts too much to even *drive* to the leisure centre. Nan says swimming would probably help soothe his joints but he won't listen.

Last year I came bronze in our school's swimming competition. I don't like to brag, but I'd hardly even practised. It's part of an end-of-year event held before the summer holidays, where our school rents a local outdoor swimming pool and holds a fete on the grassy bit nearby. There's a burger and ice-cream van, lots of stalls selling homemade things, and colourful signs and banners everywhere. We had to swim up and down the length of the pool four times as quickly as possible, and people lined up to cheer us on.

When Mr Davidson handed me my bronze medal, everyone in the crowd began clapping and cheering. As I walked around the fete with the medal round my neck and a damp towel on my shoulders, people were patting me on the back and telling me how well I'd done. It actually felt quite *nice* being the centre of attention for once, especially when I'm so used to Chloe being it all the time.

"With a bit more practice I reckon you could think about entering the regional swimming contest next year," said Mr Davidson. "Who knows – you might even win another medal."

Grandad said he'd never been so proud.

"I love this song!" squealed Neada as we drove through the town. Chloe was in charge of the radio, switching through stations before we even had a chance to hear what was being played.

"Me too," said Jess. "My brothers went to see them in concert."

I didn't know who the boy band were, but pretended I loved them as well and nodded.

"They're so lame," Chloe said. "I've told you both that before."

Neada and Jess looked at one another. Recently Chloe had become a lot bossier than usual. Even though she was being mean, they couldn't say anything back to her when Chloe's mum was in the car. I certainly wouldn't want to argue with her.

Chloe's mum quickly changed the subject. "It's that school swimming competition in a few weeks' time," she said as we pulled into the leisure centre. "I remember you doing so well last year, Molly. You got a bronze medal, didn't you? Amazing."

I nodded. I always get shy talking to Chloe's mum. She's just *so pretty*. Words seem to jumble out of my mouth and I sound silly in front of her.

I wondered if this is how some people felt when they spoke to Chloe.

"*It was only bronze,*" Chloe muttered.

"Bronze is a brilliant achievement," Chloe's mum replied, raising her eyebrow. "Why don't you think about joining the swimming club, Chloe? You always enjoyed it when you went with Molly and her grandad. It's just a shame Jack's too ill to take you both any more."

Chloe scoffed and rolled her eyes. "Yeah, right, Mum. I did that when I was seven."

"What's wrong with swimming?" her mum asked. "Swimming's great for toning. I have a friend who *swears* by it after having twins. Isn't that right, Molly?"

I didn't say anything. I wouldn't know. I only swim for fun.

"The only people in the swimming club are geeks," Chloe replied, and began to fiddle with the beading on her dress.

Chloe often has a habit of not thinking before she speaks. Sometimes it feels like she says things just to be mean. She *knows* how much I like the swimming club and the fact Mr Davidson thinks I'm good enough to start practising for regionals.

I couldn't tell if Chloe's mum wanted to tell her off or not, but, either way, she didn't seem best pleased with her.

"If you want to stay slim as you get older, you need to take up some form of exercise," her mum said, which I thought was a bit odd, considering Chloe is one of the thinnest girls in our entire school. "You can't keep eating the junk you do and expect to stay slim forever. I'm warning you now – wait and see."

"Well, swimming *obviously* doesn't make you slim. Just look at how fat Mol—" Chloe started, before stopping herself. Everyone went quiet suddenly, and it took me a couple of moments to realise who she was talking about.

Me.

3

When we got to the changing rooms at the leisure centre, Neada and I went into one cubicle, Chloe and Jess into another.

No one had really said a word since Chloe's outburst in the car, and she wasn't looking me in the eye either. Usually we'd get a changing room together, but this time she seemed overly keen to go with Jess.

I took my swimming costume out of my bag and studied it. It was strange – I knew I was a lot taller than the other girls, but I'd never thought I was that much *bigger* than them. I guess my arms and shoulders were a bit wider than the others' but that was about it.

Gabby Morris in our class is fat, but she always makes jokes about it. She's really kind – always happy and eager to help out with the school's charity events – but she really struggles to keep up in PE. She comes to school with a massive lunch box, full of chocolate and crisps and fizzy drinks, and then eats snacks in the afternoon when she thinks no one's watching.

Even though Gabby describes herself as fat, Chloe and the boys would sometimes make fun of her weight behind her back. I wondered if this was what Chloe did behind my back too. Sometimes I really don't like Chloe much at all, even if she *is* meant to be my best friend.

I watched Neada getting changed into her costume. She's a lot shorter than me, with caramel skin, beautiful shiny hair and skinny legs that almost look too long for her body. My shoulders came up to where the top of her head was.

When I thought about it properly, I suppose I *did* look fatter than the other girls. Chloe and Neada had always been thin. Jess played football a lot and had a younger brother to play with, so she was always moving. But I didn't understand why I was bigger when I exercised just as much as them, if not more.

"I don't think you're fat," Neada said out of the blue suddenly, and I quickly looked away, embarrassed that she must've seen I'd been staring at her. "Don't listen to Chloe."

I looked down. For the first time ever, I suddenly felt shy to put my costume on. Usually I couldn't wait to get in the pool, but all of a sudden I felt incredibly self-conscious. The stretchy material clung to my body like cling film. Did other people in my class think I was fat too?

We put our belongings in the locker and went to meet Chloe and Jess by the pool. Neada's slim legs looked like a model's as she walked ahead of me. Mine looked muscly and they rubbed together.

I felt better once we got to the pool. The pads of my feet grazed over the ridges in the tiles and I smelled the chlorine in the air. I couldn't wait to be under the water again to forget about what had been said.

"Where's Chloe?" Neada asked Jess, looking around the pool. Jess shrugged her shoulders.

And then, as if on cue, Chloe strolled towards us, making her grand appearance. She was wearing a tiny red bikini, her hair bouncing on her shoulders as though she was the star of her very own music video.

I hadn't noticed until now, but Chloe's chest was actually *growing*. We'd stuffed our tops with tissue paper at my house once to see what we'd look like as grown-ups, but now she was on her way to getting *proper* boobs. It was one more thing Chloe had that I didn't.

"Wow, Chloe!" Neada said. "A *bikini*! My mum would never let me wear one of those."

Chloe brushed her hair off her shoulders. "Seriously, Neada," she said, hand on hip. "We're going to secondary school in a few months. Your mum needs to realise we're not kids any more."

Neada went bright pink. But perhaps Chloe was right. If anyone knew what it was like to be a grown-up, it was Chloe. Her mum let her wear lip gloss to school, and at weekends even let her wear *mascara*. She'd had her first kiss in the playground in Year 5 and she owned her first bra at eight, even though back then she only had bee stings for a chest.

"Coming in?" Chloe said, hoisting herself down the ladder and checking to see if any boys were watching her. I saw some girls nearby looking at her enviously.

"Watch out!" Neada yelled, and jumped in from the side of the pool, making water splash everywhere like a tsunami. Chloe got completely drenched, her blonde hair clinging to her face like seaweed.

"My *hair*!" Chloe yelled, and splashed Neada back, who by this point was laughing hysterically.

We all began splashing each other, jumping under the water and screaming and laughing for what felt like hours. It was just like the old days, when Chloe didn't care about her appearance and would just be silly and fun and *nice*.

"*Oi!*" yelled a familiar voice from the side of the pool. We all stopped splashing and looked up.

Great. It was Tom Beckett and his group of friends, huddled together and laughing like they were some kind of witches' coven.

I liked to call their group "Tom and the Sheep". Whatever Tom said or did, the other boys copied or found hilarious, even when it wasn't. I hadn't seen Tom in a while and he looked a lot taller than how I remembered. They were in the year above us at school and were now at the secondary school we were going to after the summer holidays. I couldn't *stand* them.

Chloe suddenly jumped away from us in the water, combing her sopping hair with her fingers. It was almost as though she was embarrassed to be seen with us.

"Hi, Tom!" she yelled back, blushing. In a second, all the fun we'd been having drained away and Chloe was back to being annoying again.

I went to give Neada and Jess a stare, but they started blushing too. I rolled my eyes in complete disbelief. We used to make fun of Chloe for acting that way, and now here they were, acting the very same! Neada had never mentioned boys before so I don't know why she was acting all giddy around them. And Jess was always *one* of the boys, not the type to actually fancy them.

Without saying a word, the three of them swam over quickly to speak to Tom and the Sheep. I couldn't believe it. We always used to make fun of how immature Tom and his friends were, and now here my friends were, actually *talking* to them.

I stood in the middle of the pool, feeling stupid

at being left on my own, and also feeling stupid for feeling jealous about being left.

"Who's your mate, Chloe?" I heard Tom ask, and the Sheep looked at me in unison. I glared back at him, trying to look as annoyed as possible. We'd been having a great time until he and his stupid friends ruined it for us.

I decided I'd go and practise my diving instead. I swam over to the steps, listening to Chloe, Neada and Jess laughing hysterically at something particularly unfunny Tom had said.

As I climbed out of the pool I took one more look behind me. No wonder the boys wanted to talk to the girls. They looked so pretty and dainty standing there in their costumes. Even if I did join them, I'd probably embarrass them somehow. Unlike Chloe, I'm not confident speaking in front of new groups of people, *especially* not lots of boys. It was better I kept to myself.

I climbed the ladder and stood on the edge of the diving board, arms raised above my head like a ballerina. And then, in my mind, I was an Olympic athlete, about to perform the best dive the world had ever seen, with hundreds of people in the stadium chanting my name.

Moll-y! Moll-y! Moll-y! Moll-y!

Until I realised that people *were* chanting at me.

"*Jump, whale, jump!*" Tom yelled from across the pool, his voice echoing across the tiles.

Suddenly I snapped out of my daydream. All I could hear was the sound of endless laughter rippling across the water and I wished I could dive into a pool of darkness, never to be seen again.

4

I didn't stay for the rest of Chloe's party. I couldn't face it. I ran into the changing rooms, trying my hardest not to cry, and called Nan from the cheap mobile she'd bought me for emergencies.

"Everything all right?" Nan answered, sounding slightly panicked.

"I feel really ill, Nan," I lied, my voice wobbling. "I was almost sick in the pool. I really don't want to ruin the rest of Chloe's birthday. Can you please come and pick me up?"

Chloe, Neada and Jess followed me into the changing room and begged me not to go. Chloe said I'd ruin the rest of her birthday if I left, but I lied to them too, saying I felt poorly. It wasn't a *total* lie, because the shame made me feel as though I had a million butterflies trapped in my tummy, beating hard against my ribcage.

I'd never been more embarrassed in my life. All I could think about was Tom Beckett yelling *"Jump, whale, jump!"* over and over in my head.

The girls waited with me outside for Nan to arrive. Neada put her arm round my shoulders and Jess linked her arm through mine. Chloe huffed and puffed and kept complaining about how selfish I was being.

Seeing Nan's car pull up in the car park made me feel as though I was being rescued. I ran to the car as quickly as I could, heart thumping beneath my jumper at the thought of seeing Tom and the Sheep again. I just wanted to go *home*.

Nan asked what I wanted for tea but I was too upset to eat. I think she knew I wasn't *really* ill but she didn't say anything. She wrapped me up in a blanket on the sofa, made me a hot chocolate and we watched some silly game shows on TV with Grandad until I went upstairs to bed.

I cried and cried and cried that night. I tried to be quiet so that Nan and Grandad wouldn't hear me, but I sobbed into my pillow until my face felt hot and my eyes turned puffy.

I couldn't remember ever crying as much as this. I *never* cry. Grandad says I've never cried as much as the day my mum left, as we watched her climb into the passenger side of her new boyfriend's car and drive off down the road.

I don't know much about my mum at all. I don't know what she does for a job, or what her house is like, or what her favourite colour is. I don't remember a lot about her at all, except for the smell of a fancy perfume she used to wear that she'd left in Nan and Grandad's bathroom cabinet.

I have a photo of her on my bedside table but she might as well be a stranger. She's pretty – not as pretty as Chloe's mum, but still good-looking – with lots of piercings in her ears and long, light-brown hair that almost comes down to her waist. She's laughing and wearing a leather jacket, sitting on a wall outside without a care in the world.

Grandad says she's not "fit to be a mother", which I find a bit odd, as in every photo I've seen of her she looks very slim. Nan says he shouldn't say things like that about his own daughter but Grandad says he doesn't care. He says it would take her two minutes to send an email or a text – two minutes to let us know she's alive and well. I used to get postcards from her sometimes but I haven't in a long time. I'd actually rather she never wrote to me again, because then I could forget about her completely, instead of getting my hopes up.

I wonder what my life would've been like if she'd raised me properly. Maybe we'd have gone on fun adventures around the world together – trekking through the jungle with exotic animals for pets, or having dinner over coal fires and dancing with ancient tribes. I could be homeschooled by her, so I'd never have to deal with mean people like Chloe or Tom Beckett again. And then we'd write a book about our amazing adventures together, selling millions of copies across the globe, where girls would feel envious of our special mother–daughter bond.

I bet she'd be a lot more relaxed with certain things than Nan is. She'd probably be like Chloe's mum, letting me do whatever I want and buying me presents. From what I've heard, she seems very

carefree and easy-going. Maybe a bit *too* much …
but mums are meant to be fun, aren't they?

Nan woke me up on Sunday morning. She sat on
the edge of my bed with a cup of tea and shook
me gently, but I was already awake.

"I thought we could go for breakfast at the café
down the road," she said. "My treat. You must be
starving by now, poor thing."

I was so upset by what had been said yesterday
that I hadn't thought about food in the slightest,
but I love eating at the café with Nan. It's always
such a treat. We order big fried breakfasts that
we can never finish, and sometimes I'm allowed a
milkshake as well. If Nan was trying to cheer me
up, it was working.

"Nan," I asked as we headed down the road.
"Can I ask you something?"

"Anything," she replied. "You know that."

I took a deep breath. "Do you think I'm fat?"

Nan glanced down at me and laughed loudly.
"You?! *Fat?*" she said. "Of course not. Why, did
someone say something to you?"

"No," I lied, although I'm not a very good liar.
My voice suddenly went high-pitched. "No. I just

feel fat compared to Chloe, Neada and Jess. They're just so … so…"

"Petite?" Nan replied.

I guessed "petite" was a posh word for looking small. "Yes. Petite."

"They're just built differently to you," she said. "You're a lot taller than them and your shoulders are broader, but that doesn't mean you're *fat*. All girls are built differently."

I wanted to argue and tell her she was wrong – that both Chloe and Tom had said things about my weight in the space of a few hours, so it must've been true. But I didn't want to upset her. Nan had once had a row with Chloe's mum after Chloe had made me cry at school and I didn't want her doing it again.

"There's a big difference between being taller and bigger than someone and being fat," she said. "We eat healthy meals at home and you exercise." She raised an eyebrow at me. "I hope this isn't something you've read about in a magazine or seen on the telly."

I rarely looked at magazines – Nan's weekly ones were so boring and always had stupid stories in them – and I certainly didn't compare myself to anyone in them or on TV. In fact, until Chloe had said I was fat in the car, I'd honestly never compared my body to *anyone*. My body was just that: *a body*.

"Neada's family are all tiny people," she continued. "She'll never be tall like you. Someone like Jess is built for running, because she has long legs. And Chloe's mum and dad are both slim, so she's bound to look that way." She grabbed on to my arm protectively as we crossed the road. "None of them have got strong arms or legs like you. They'll never be able to swim the way you do, but I bet they wish they could. You have a swimmer's body! And that's why you do so well at it."

We sat in our favourite spot by the café window and Nan picked up a copy of the Sunday paper. There was a fashion magazine in the middle, so she handed it to me and began reading something about a footballer kissing someone he shouldn't have.

The women smiling back at me from the pages of the magazine had the sort of bodies Neada, Chloe and Jess had – *thin*. They were wearing the prettiest clothes and the highest heels. Their teeth were perfectly symmetrical and their hair was the shiniest I'd ever seen. But no matter how much I flicked through the magazine, no one inside had a body shaped like mine.

"Why don't I look like these women?" I asked Nan, holding the magazine up in front of her face. Nan wrapped her hands around her tea and looked at me over her glasses.

"*Those* women don't look like those women," she said, her forehead knitting into a frown. "They're models. They're all airbrushed on a computer to look that way. You can remove their spots in an instant, or give them a thinner waist or bigger boobs, all with the click of a mouse. And even if they *are* that thin in real life, a lot of them are miserable trying to stay that way."

"What do you mean?" I asked.

"They'll stop eating just to fit into clothes," she said. "Imagine that! Not eating anything nice because you want to fit into a skirt or pair of jeans."

I had to admit – that didn't sound much fun.

"I'll tell you one thing," she said. "I'd rather look a bit bigger, eat nice meals and be *happy*. Worrying about what you look like all the time doesn't sound like much of a life at all."

5

I dreaded waking up on Monday morning for school. I *really* didn't want to face the girls and have them bring up what had happened at the weekend. Chloe must've thought I was the biggest baby in the world for leaving her party early and not talking to the boys like the others had.

What if she'd told everyone else in class about what Tom Beckett had said to me? The last thing I wanted was the rest of the school finding out and making fun of me too. My tummy was doing somersaults as I walked up to the school gates. I pictured people standing on both sides of the corridor, laughing at me like an animal in a circus.

No one said anything as I hurried up the school path. They didn't say anything as I raced down the school corridor. In fact, nobody batted an eyelid at me at all.

Neada and Jess were acting friendlier towards me than usual though, waving to me as I walked through the classroom door. They bounced over, linking arms with mine on either side.

"Are you feeling any better, Mol?" Jess asked. "We really missed you at Chloe's."

"It wasn't the same without you there," said Neada. "It was a bit boring, actually."

"Chloe was really bossy," Jess added. "And the takeaway wasn't very nice either."

I nodded and gave them a faint smile. I knew they knew I wasn't *really* ill, but I was so glad they weren't bringing up what Tom and the Sheep had said. And it certainly made me feel a lot better to think I'd been missed at the party, whether or not Chloe felt the same way.

Chloe arrived late to class. She came and sat at our table and threw her bag noisily on the floor. Mrs Ingram raised her eyebrows at her disapprovingly and tutted.

"You missed a great sleepover," she whispered to me, pulling out her pencil case. "Wasn't it great, guys?"

Neada and Jess nodded sheepishly.

"We stayed up till three in the morning watching films," Chloe said. "It was so much fun, wasn't it, guys? You really missed out."

"Quiet, Chloe," Mrs Ingram said, and the three of us stared down into our notebooks.

I was on my way to lunch with Chloe when I heard someone call my name.

"Molly!"

It was Mr Davidson, my swimming teacher, dressed in a navy tracksuit and carrying his PE kit over one shoulder.

"Do you have a moment to chat?" he asked. "It's about the swimming regionals that are coming up."

Chloe looked at me with a smug expression on her face. *Great.* Discussing swimming regionals was the *last* thing I needed to chat about after the weekend, especially in front of her.

I really didn't want Chloe to think I was a baby any more.

"I'm a bit busy for swimming club, actually," I replied cockily, folding my arms. Chloe sniggered. Unlike her, I'd never spoken to a teacher like that before and I wasn't sure where it had come from. It didn't sound like me at all.

Mr Davidson did not seem pleased. I regretted what I'd said instantly.

"Do you mind if I speak to Molly alone, please?" he asked, turning to Chloe. It was clear from his tone that Chloe didn't have a say in the matter, and Chloe usually has an answer for everything.

"Erm ... OK. See you at lunch, Molly," she said, and wandered off, looking over her shoulder a few times to see if she was missing out on anything important.

"Molly," he said, turning to me. "I know looking cool in front of your friends seems like the most important thing in the world right now, but trust me – it isn't. You have such a great talent. Why would you want to throw that away?"

I didn't want to throw anything away, especially not a swimming competition. The thing was, I *knew* Mr Davidson was right but I didn't want to be a laughing stock at the pool again. And although Chloe couldn't care less about how she spoke to people, I felt bad for being rude.

"I do know that it's hard for you to get to the extra training sessions in the mornings," he said, before I'd even had a chance to reply. "And I was wondering – if it's OK with you, of course – whether I could ask your grandparents about driving you to practice myself? I already drive Ed in the mornings and I think it would be a great way for you to improve."

I wanted to scream "*YES!*" at the top of my voice so that the whole world could hear. Going to morning swimming practices with the others was all I'd wanted to do for such a long time. I often felt I missed out on special in-jokes and other stories that Ed and the group shared when I saw them on Wednesday evenings.

But another part of me was worried about being seen in my swimming costume again. And I worried about Chloe not thinking I was cool enough. I needed Chloe to be onside when we went to St Margaret's, just like she'd been throughout primary school. After all, Neada and Jess were best friends and could depend on each other. *My* supposed best friend was Chloe. And putting up with some of the mean things Chloe said or did was *much* better than being alone.

"We only have a few weeks left to practise before regionals," he said. "But just think – if you managed to win a bronze with hardly any practice, imagine what you could win with a bit more?"

Grandad would be ecstatic if I won another competition. I desperately wanted to make him happy. But I also wanted to stay in Chloe's good books. What was I going to do?

Then an idea came to me. What if I went to practices in secret? They started at seven in the morning. Chloe would never need to know I'd been. I'd still arrive to school at the same time in the mornings. She'd never know about me competing in the regional swimming contest either – it wasn't being held in school or at the leisure centre we went to on her birthday. And best of all, Grandad would be proud of me too.

It was the best idea I'd ever had. It was a win–win situation!

"OK, Mr Davidson," I replied. "I'm sure my nan would be fine with that."

As I sat down to lunch, Chloe leaned over to me.

"What did Mr Davidson want?" she asked nosily,

munching on her crisps.

"Oh, just about competing in some lame swimming competition with the club," I replied, trying to sound as unbothered as possible.

I watched a look of awkwardness creep up on Neada's and Jess's faces. As much as I wanted them to, they clearly hadn't forgotten about what Tom had said on Saturday.

"Don't worry though," I said quickly, trying to sound upbeat. "I'm over swimming now. It's like you said, Chloe. Swimming club is for babies and geeks."

I smiled at them and bit into my sandwich, trying to make the atmosphere a bit less tense. I didn't want them thinking I was still hurting from the other day. Neada and Jess looked at one another, but they didn't say anything.

"God, look at Gabby Morris," Chloe whispered, and we all turned to look. She was sitting alone again, eating her lunch.

"Shouldn't we invite her over to come and sit with us?" I asked. "I feel bad that she's eating on her own."

"She looks sad," Neada said. "I'd hate to sit on my own."

"Me too," said Jess. "I'll go and ask her to join us." She stood up and went to leave the table.

"Jess, *no!*" Chloe hissed, grabbing her arm fiercely. "We don't want to be seen with *her!* We'll never live it down. She's just so ... so ... *embarrassing.*"

Jess looked at Chloe with a mixture of anger and disappointment. She clearly wanted to say something back at her, but instead she just slunk back in her seat. Neada would never stand up to Chloe, and I wouldn't either. But in that moment I felt like a total coward for not doing so.

"Guys," Chloe said. "I know you think I'm being a total cow for saying that, but you have to understand. We could be the *coolest* girls joining St Margaret's! We could be the girls that all the other girls want to be and who all the boys want to go out with. All of that preparation starts *now*. And that means choosing the people you're seen with carefully."

If being cool meant hanging around with Chloe, and being mean to other people, I wasn't entirely sure I wanted to be her friend at all.

6

Grandad opened the door when I got home from school that night with a massive grin on his face.

"I've just spoken to Mr Davidson!" he said, giving me a hug. "How exciting!"

Grandad felt frailer to me than usual. He didn't have the round tummy he once had and was using a stick to walk with that the doctor had given him recently.

"What's this about?" Nan asked, closing the door behind us and putting her bag on the side.

"Mr Davidson rang to ask if he can drive Molly to morning swimming practices," Grandad told her. "I think it's a great idea. He really thinks you can go far with this swimming, Molly. I'm so proud of you!"

It was the happiest I'd seen Grandad look in a long time. His cheeks were all rosy and his eyes shone brightly. At that moment, I didn't care about impressing Chloe. I just wanted to make him happy.

"You'll have to get up early," he said. "Mr Davidson says you'll feel exhausted from the training. It won't be easy. Do you think you can do it?"

I nodded. "I really want to do it, Grandad," I said. "Please let me go!"

"I've already told him you can. He's picking you up at six thirty tomorrow morning. Then he'll drop you and Ed off afterwards at the breakfast club in school."

I was so excited. I couldn't wait to see Ed and the others. I was going to make sure I won another medal if it was the last thing I did.

I was walking to the bathroom to brush my teeth that night when I heard Nan talking on the phone in her bedroom. No one ever rang this late. The door was ajar slightly, the gentle glow from her bedside lamp pouring out on to the carpet in the corridor. I peeped through the slit in the door, trying to be as quiet as a mouse, and saw her sitting on the edge of the bed.

"I don't care, Angela," I heard her say on the phone, fiddling with the phone cord. "Your father is very ill. It might be nice if you weren't so selfish for once and came and saw him. Or your daughter, for that matter."

Angela? There was only one Angela I knew.

"She has a big swimming competition in a few weeks," Nan whispered. "It's against other children from different schools in the county. Why don't you come and watch her? She's so good at it – a real water baby. Her PE teacher thinks she'll do really well."

I couldn't stop myself. I swung open the door and jumped into the room excitedly.

"*Mum!*" I yelled, and went to grab the phone. I wanted to tell her about the swimming contest myself. Nan sighed, loosening her grip on the phone awkwardly, as though she didn't want me speaking to her.

"Hello?" I said, hoping she was still there. I hadn't

spoken to my mum in the longest time. I bet she missed me a lot. She was probably a successful businesswoman, making millions across the world and too busy to chat on the phone or to write letters.

"Hi, Molly," she replied.

Mum's voice sounded more hoarse than I remembered. It didn't match up with the photo I had of her in my room. She didn't sound young and carefree. She didn't sound very well at all.

"Are you ill, Mum?" I asked. I couldn't think what else to say. What *do* you say to someone you don't really know?

"I'm fine," she said, although I could tell that she wasn't. "So what's this about swimming? Nan says you're really good at it."

I told her all about swimming classes and how much fun I had with my boy-friend-but-not-*boyfriend* Ed. I told her that I was going to start training in the mornings with Mr Davidson. I told her I wanted to be a famous swimmer and win competitions across the world. I didn't tell her about Tom Beckett calling me a whale.

Mum didn't seem that interested in my swimming. It was almost like she wasn't listening at all.

"What year are you in again?" she asked croakily. "Do you have a boyfriend yet?"

"I'm in Year Six," I said. *Why didn't she know that?* I spotted Nan glance at me and then look away again. "And no, I don't have one," I said quietly. "Boys are *soooo* annoying."

"Oh," she said. There was a bit of a silence on the phone, and I didn't know what else to say.

"Er ... so do you think you can come to watch me compete?" I asked hopefully. "You can watch with Nan and Grandad in the audience. I'm going to train so hard for it."

Nan reached over my shoulder and grabbed the phone from out of my hands.

"Angela, we'll talk to you soon," she said. "Do try coming. We'd all like to see you."

And then she hung up.

I was so annoyed at Nan for doing that. I was trying to have a nice conversation with my mum and she'd completely spoiled it!

"What did you do that for?" I said crossly. "I can't believe you hung up on her! She probably won't come at all now!"

"Your mum is an adult, Molly," she said. "It's

41

up to her whether she decides to come or not. Don't get your hopes up. Your grandfather and I certainly don't."

I couldn't believe Nan was being such a cow.

"Why do you have to ruin everything?" I yelled, and stormed into my room.

Nan walked across the landing to the bathroom. I could've been wrong, but it sounded to me like she was crying.

7

Waking up at the crack of dawn was not my idea of fun at all. My eyes felt all groggy and heavy.

"Come on, Mol!" Grandad whispered, trying not to wake Nan. He turned my bedroom light on, which made my eyes sting even more. I groaned. It was six in the morning. *Why on earth had I agreed to this?*

I put my dressing gown on and went downstairs. Grandad poured me a bowl of rice crispies and made me a cup of tea.

"I thought I was going to the breakfast club with Ed afterwards?" I said, as he plodded around the kitchen with his stick.

"You can't go swimming on an empty stomach. You need all the energy you can get."

I wasn't in the mood to eat, but I ate the cereal and drank my tea anyway. Grandad had already packed my swimming kit for me the night before. I brushed my teeth and waited downstairs by the window for Mr Davidson to arrive.

Sure enough, Mr Davidson pulled up outside in his beaten-up blue car at six thirty on the dot. It was still a bit dark outside, with the glow of a few street lamps lighting up the pavement. I watched as a couple of people got into their cars to go to work. I wasn't used to the street being this silent.

"*Molly!*" Ed yelled from out of the car window and started waving his arms excitedly.

"Ssh, Ed!" said Mr Davidson. "People are still in bed."

I giggled. Ed always makes me laugh. For a boy, he's quite funny, I guess. At school he's the class clown and always does silly things to make us laugh, even the teachers. If he wasn't a boy, I'd *much* rather he was my best friend than Chloe.

Chloe isn't always nice to Ed. If he ever says hi to me in class she'll roll her eyes at him and pull me away. Neada and Jess think he's funny too, but Chloe says he's ridiculously immature so we're not allowed to talk to him.

Grandad gave me a kiss and I walked down the path towards the car. It felt a bit strange being in a car with a teacher. I handed Mr Davidson Grandad's permission slip and we drove off, Grandad waving goodbye from inside the doorway.

"Are you excited about swimming?" Ed asked, turning round to look at me and grinning. He always looks a bit scruffy, with brown hair that falls over his eyes, and oversized clothes. "I was so excited when Mr Davidson said you were coming."

"I can't wait," I replied, forcing a smile, though deep down I was very nervous about being seen in my costume again. Even though Ed had never said anything about my body, he was a boy. What if he secretly thought I was a whale too?

I went into the changing room and began to change into my costume. Even though I was on my own, I felt more exposed than ever.

Unlike Chloe's, my chest was as flat as an ironing board and my shoulders wide and broad. I wished I could just enjoy swimming again, without worrying about what I looked like. Just last week, I had no idea my body shape was so horrendous. I hated Chloe and Tom Beckett for making me feel this way.

I must've been sat in the changing room for a long time, because there was suddenly a loud knock on the door.

"Molly!" Mr Davidson yelled. "Are you in there? I'll send Alice to come and get you in a minute."

"Coming!" I yelled back, grabbing my stuff quickly and shoving it in an empty locker. I wrapped a towel round my waist, making sure I hid my tummy, and went outside to meet the others.

"There you are," he said. "You took your time. Get in the pool and start warming up with the others."

Everyone in the team was so happy to see me. They were already stretching in the water, looking like funny aliens in their tight swimming caps and goggles. No one looked at my body any differently as I hoisted myself slowly into the water.

"Hi, Molly!" yelled Alice from the water.

Alice is our club's captain and is by far the best

swimmer I've ever seen. She's a few years older than us but helps out at our club because her dad says it will look good for when she applies to university. She always seems to be in our local paper and everybody knows who she is. She enters swimming competitions all across England and wins lots of medals and certificates, but has to get up really early every day to train – even at weekends.

If I could be like anyone, it would be Alice. I wish I could win competitions like her. I wish I was as popular as her. I even wish I could look like her. She has strong arms and strong legs, and people take notice of her when she's racing because she's so fast.

"Right, listen up, everyone," Mr Davidson said, and we all gathered round. "Regionals are in eight weeks' time. That may sound like a long way away, but it's not. You've all got great potential and we still have a lot of training to do, but I really want us to win some more medals for the club this year."

Ed leaned over. "I bet you'll win another medal," he whispered into my ear, and I smiled, crossing my fingers under the water in hope.

Mr Davidson put us into partners, ready for our first race. Thankfully I was teamed with Ed. I would've hated to have been paired up with someone I didn't know.

We were going to do a relay race, jumping from the platforms at the end of the pool, swimming as fast as we could to the other end and back before switching with the other swimmer.

It was Ed's turn first. He put his goggles on and stuck his thumb up at me. I stuck mine up in return. I so desperately wanted to win – I didn't want to let him or Mr Davidson down. I wanted to make a great first impression at my first proper practice session.

"*Three … two … one!*" Mr Davidson yelled.

SPLASH!!!

There was a sudden flurry of bodies throwing themselves into the water. Alice and Mr Davidson were clapping and cheering from the side.

"Faster!" yelled Alice.

"Come on!" yelled Mr Davidson.

Ed was in the lead. I cheered for him as he splashed his way down the pool, his arms whirling like turbines, occasionally coming up for air.

Before I knew it, Ed was quickly approaching

me. My palms felt sweaty, ready to dive in past the red-headed girl next to me. *I wasn't going to let Mr Davidson down, I wasn't going to let Mr Davidson down, I wasn't going to let Mr Davidson down...*

Ed was still in first place. He kept swimming faster and faster towards me and I reached my hands up, ready to dive in as soon as he reached the platform.

But it was as though my body had turned to jelly. All of a sudden I wobbled on the platform, losing my balance, my hands flopping in the air, and before I knew it...

"*Ahhh!*" I squealed, and toppled into the water like a pancake. The redhead next to me was already on her way by this point, and I was left trying to catch up from what felt like miles behind.

I came last. I couldn't believe it. I'd always been the most confident swimmer and now it was like I'd never been in the pool in my life.

"Don't worry," Alice said, putting her arm round my shoulder. "It's only your first real practice session. You'll be a star, I'm sure of it."

By the weekend I was exhausted. I'd woken up

at five thirty three mornings in a row, gone to school all day *and* been to my usual swimming class on Wednesday night. My calves felt heavy and swollen, as though there were bags of sugar in them, and my arms ached too much to pick anything up. All I wanted to do was *sleep*.

Chloe, Neada and Jess had no idea I'd been practising in secret. Keeping that from them was tiring in itself. I was pretty sure Neada and Jess wouldn't care about me swimming – they might have even been supportive – but I couldn't risk Chloe finding out.

Each morning I'd make sure my hair was bone-dry before I went back to school. Before I saw anyone in class, I'd hide my swimming kit deep inside my locker so no one would smell the chlorine. As far as Chloe was concerned, I'd given swimming up for good.

If only she knew the fun I was having. Swimming was definitely tough but I was having the *best* time with Ed. He was a lot more fun than Chloe, that's for sure. He made me cry tears of laughter with his silly impressions and funny jokes, making me laugh until my tummy muscles hurt.

The only thing I didn't like was having to avoid

him in school for fear of Chloe finding out my secret. I would quickly look away if he ever tried to make eye contact. Chloe said he was the uncoolest boy in the year, and I didn't want her thinking I was associating with him. I just wanted her to like me.

Over the next couple of weeks swimming practices gradually seemed to blur into one. All my efforts were going into making sure I was fast enough for regionals and trying to keep everyone around me happy. My life felt like one big balancing act.

Grandad was happy with me. Nan said he looked the brightest he had in a long time. He'd squeeze my arms and call me Popeye like the cartoon character, joking about how big my muscles were getting, and he would proudly mention my swimming competition whenever anyone called the house.

Mr Davidson seemed happy with me too. Although he said my swimming was improving after every practice, it sometimes felt that no matter how much I pushed myself, he'd yell at me to swim faster. Half of me would be annoyed at him for pushing me so much, yet the other half was desperate for him to tell me I'd done a good job.

There was only one person who didn't seem that happy with me.

Despite the fact she'd seemed OK since I'd pretended to give up swimming, Chloe's attitude towards me began changing again. I didn't understand what I was doing wrong. I was trying my absolute best to fit in but Chloe always seemed irritated with me. Had she discovered my secret?

I'd make jokes and she wouldn't laugh – just roll her eyes or stay quiet. She'd ask to sit next to Neada or Jess in class, when we'd *always* sat together. *What was I doing wrong?*

I wondered if my appearance had anything to do with it. I liked being in school because it meant we were all dressed in the same uniform. But at weekends it had become more awkward. Chloe told me I needed to change the way I dressed because I "looked like a five-year-old", and that she wouldn't be seen in public with me until I did.

Over the past few weeks Jess and Neada had both started buying fashionable new clothes. They looked like models, and I couldn't help but feel jealous that their mums took them shopping at the weekends and spoiled them rotten. Nan never did that with me because she was too busy working all the time. I couldn't help but feel left out when the three of them sat around chatting about the latest things they'd bought and the newest fashion trends.

I decided I needed to keep Chloe sweet. I persuaded Nan to drive me to Riverdale, the local shopping centre, to buy me some new clothes that I knew Chloe would approve of. If dressing better meant Chloe would be my friend, it was worth a shot.

We'd been wandering around the shopping centre for a while when I suddenly saw the most perfect dress on a hanger. It was short and red with stars all over. It looked so grown-up. Neada had something similar in her wardrobe and Chloe had said how cool it was. I was certain that if I bought a dress like that, Chloe would think I was cool too.

"It's a bit skimpy," Nan said in the changing room, frowning slightly. "I'm not sure I want you walking round the town like that."

"But Chloe *always* wears stuff like this," I said,

frustrated. "Even Neada does, and you know what her mum is like."

It just wasn't fair. Chloe's mum seemed to buy her new clothes every week. I couldn't even remember the last time I'd had anything new.

I begged Nan for the dress.

"*Pleeaaasseeeeee!*" I said, putting my hands together and batting my eyelashes at her. It was the prettiest dress I'd ever seen.

"It's very expensive, Molly," she said, looking at the label. "And I doubt your grandad would be happy if you wore that out. So it's a no, I'm afraid."

I was so disappointed as I watched the sales assistant take it away. I was sick of being the one person in our group who was dressed like a baby at weekends, like the stupid dungarees I was always made to wear. If everything was as expensive as she moaned about, why couldn't Nan just get a better job?

We settled for two new tops and a skirt instead. It was better than nothing, but they weren't as grown-up as I'd have liked.

I think Nan knew I was disappointed, because that night she went out and got us some fish and chips for dinner. It didn't give me the same feeling that buying the beautiful dress would have, exactly, but it did cheer me up.

We had a really good time round the dinner table that night. Even Nan looked like she was having fun, joining in with my and Grandad's jokes, and laughing. Grandad began telling us stories of when he'd been an athlete, using the ketchup bottle as a replica of him for effect. He told us all the naughty things he and his friends would get up to when they were young, like stealing apples from the vicar's garden.

As we laughed, I felt bad for being a brat about the dress. I realised I really do love Nan and Grandad, even if they are a bit overprotective sometimes.

Someone rang the doorbell, so Nan got up to answer it. Grandad's stories were getting funnier and funnier – one time he'd even been in trouble with the police for playing Knock Down Ginger!

And then suddenly our lovely evening took a very unexpected turn.

8

"Angela!" Nan gasped, her voice sounding a mixture of surprised, overwhelmed and confused, all at the same time. "What are you doing here?"

Mum looked *nothing* like how I remembered. Her hair wasn't long and shiny like it was in the photo I had of her. It looked ... well ... *dull*.

The skin around her eyes was grey and tired, and her cheeks weren't as plump as they once were. She was wearing scruffy jeans and carrying an overnight bag, as though she was planning on staying.

Grandad hobbled out of the kitchen to see

Mum for himself. It had been such a long time since we last saw her that it almost felt as though we were looking at a ghost. No one really knew what to say.

"Well, aren't you happy to see me?" she asked, dumping her bag on the floor.

I didn't know how I felt. I wasn't sure how to act around her either. Was I supposed to run and hug her? Give her a kiss, maybe? I'd seen films where kids ran into their parents' arms and then they lived happily ever after, but this wasn't a film. It was real life, and the thought of hugging someone I didn't know made me feel ... uneasy.

Grandad didn't say anything. He turned away and walked into the living room with his stick. There was an awkward silence where the three of us – me, Mum and Nan – just looked at one another, like a stand-off in an old Western film, but without the guns.

"I'll make us all a cup of tea," Nan said, and went into the kitchen, leaving Mum and me alone in the hallway together.

Even though Mum was supposed to be the adult, in that moment it felt as though I was the grown-up. She was looking at the ceiling, avoiding any sort of eye contact with me.

I noticed I was almost the same height as her. She looked a lot taller in the photo. She was small and looked a bit fragile, like she could break at any moment.

"Are you staying here?" I asked after a few seconds, glancing at her overnight bag.

"That's what I was hoping," she replied in her croaky voice. She looked down at the floor. "And I was also hoping we could get to know each other a bit better. You know, make up for lost time."

That's what I wanted more than anything. I'd dreamed about this day for years and years. I wanted someone to go shopping with and tell secrets to and help teach me about make-up, just like Chloe's mum did with her. Nan wasn't good with any of those things. She was always too busy working or doing boring things like ironing.

"Oh, before I forget," she said, fumbling around in her bag. "I've got you a little something."

I couldn't remember Mum ever buying me a single thing. She hadn't been there for any Christmases or birthdays. Some years she'd send a card, and others she'd forget entirely.

"Here you go," she said, smiling, and handed

me a gift bag. It was a bit scuffed around the edges but I didn't care. The fact she'd got me a present was something in itself.

I rustled inside and pulled out a small box.

"A *phone*!" I said, gasping.

It wasn't just any phone. It was the newest smartphone, brand new and boxed. I couldn't believe it. No one in my class had it – it had just been released. Not even Chloe, who seemed to get a new phone all the time. Nan had always said that I wasn't allowed a proper smartphone until I was thirteen – just the cheap one she'd lent me for emergencies – but I suppose my mum had more authority over what I could or couldn't have.

"*Nan!*" I yelled, and ran into the kitchen to show her. "Look what Mum got me!"

I waved the box in front of her excitedly. I know it sounds horrible, but part of me wanted to rub in the fact Mum had got me a phone when Nan said I couldn't have one.

"That's ... lovely, Mol," she said through gritted teeth. I could tell she wasn't happy but I didn't care. "Why don't you both sit with Grandad in the living room and I'll bring the tea in?"

I went to show Grandad my phone and Mum

sat on the edge of the sofa awkwardly. I broke the seal on the box and took the phone out delicately, holding it up to the light as though it was a priceless antique.

Grandad peered over his glasses.

"Where did you get the money for that?" he asked Mum.

I couldn't believe he was asking her that kind of question. He was being so *rude*. She was obviously a very successful businesswoman who had made enough money to buy these sorts of things. *That's* why she hadn't been in contact with me. Businesswomen never have time to speak to anyone. That's a fact. He was just ruining the whole atmosphere and it was starting to get on my nerves.

"Well, I love it," I said. "It's the best present I've ever, *ever* had. Thank you, Mum."

I leaned over and hugged her hard. She smiled at me, though I could almost feel Grandad's eyes staring at her through the back of my head.

Nan came in with cups of tea and biscuits on a tray, which she placed on the coffee table.

"So where's that boyfriend of yours?" Grandad asked. "What was his name again? Mark?

Michael?"

"Matt. We broke up," Mum said. "It wasn't working out."

"Probably for the best then," said Nan, trying to make polite conversation. She sat in between Mum and me on the sofa and put her hand on my leg.

"He was a total waste of space," Grandad said. "Don't know why you bothered with him in the first place." He stared at the TV, though I knew he wasn't watching it properly.

Mum looked offended.

"Are you planning on staying then?" he asked. "Or are you going to leave and not talk to us for years again?"

Mum wriggled awkwardly in her seat.

"I have nowhere else to go, Dad," she answered quietly.

"So you thought you'd come back here like we're running some sort of hotel? We're raising your daughter because *you're* too busy gallivanting from one man to the next. We took on a massive responsibility when you left. Where have you been all these years?"

Suddenly I felt like a burden – that Nan and

Grandad didn't really want me staying there with them.

"What are you doing here exactly, Angela?" he continued. "You can't just waltz in here whenever your latest relationship doesn't work out. You can't just use us whenever it's convenient for you. And you most certainly can't walk back into Molly's life whenever it suits you either."

"Fine, I'll leave then," she said, and stood up.

Both Nan and I said "Stop!" at the same time.

I really didn't want her to leave. I wanted her to stay and be my mum.

"Don't go," Nan said. She looked at Grandad pleadingly. "Come on, Jack. Let's all just calm down and have a nice evening. For Molly's sake, at least."

"Fine," Grandad said. "But if I get a whiff of anything dodgy going on here, I want her out."

"I won't let you down," Mum said, and for the first time ever, I believed her.

9

"Wow!" Neada and Jess said in unison when I held my phone out in front of them the next day.

Chloe raised her eyebrows. For someone who always had something to say, she was unusually quiet.

"Where did you get the money from for that?" she asked, although there was a part of her voice that seemed quite impressed with me as well.

"My mum bought me it," I replied, trying to sound as casual as I possibly could.

"You don't talk a lot about your mum," Jess said. "I don't think you've ever said anything about her before. Is she rich then?"

"Yes," I said. "She's a really successful businesswoman, actually. She's been away working, which is why I've been staying with my nan and grandad. And now she's coming to live with us forever."

"That's so exciting," Neada said. "Your mum sounds really cool."

Chloe knew Mum had left years ago but she didn't say anything. I felt as though I might be in her good books again.

Everyone in class wanted to look at my phone. They were passing it round and taking pictures on it. I was a bit worried about Ed holding it because he can be quite clumsy, but he was very delicate with it. Mrs Ingram told everyone to pipe down or she'd put the phone away in her desk until the end of the day.

But, best of all, Chloe wanted to sit next to me in class again! She passed me notes under the table and whispered jokes in my ear. It was quickly becoming the best day *ever*.

I couldn't wait to get to the canteen for lunch. Since I'd started training I'd been ravenously hungry. *Nothing* seemed to fill me up properly. The food behind the counter looked like jewels in a treasure chest, practically *begging* me to taste them. I'd come home after school and eat biscuits and sweets from the treats cupboard when Nan was out of the room. I'd have double helpings of dinner and something chocolatey for dessert. Alice said I was bound to feel this way because all that exercise makes you want to eat everything in sight, especially sugary things.

I was queuing up for lunch when I felt a tap on my shoulder. It was Ed, looking scruffy as usual, his tie lopsided and school jumper covered in some sort of food stain.

I glanced around, hoping Chloe wasn't watching. Thankfully she was too busy talking to a group of boys from our class to notice.

"Hi, Ed!" I said. He might have been scruffy but he actually looked … *handsome*.

I couldn't believe I'd just thought that. I looked away quickly, hoping he couldn't read minds.

Ed seemed more jittery than usual. He was fiddling with the sleeve of his jumper.

"I was wondering…" he said, glancing down at the floor. "Erm … well…"

I couldn't understand why his words weren't coming out properly.

"What, Ed?"

"What does he want?" I heard a voice say. It was Chloe, appearing at the most inconvenient moment. "Come on, Molly."

"I'm trying to talk to Molly on my own," Ed replied, glaring at her.

If Chloe was ever rude to Ed, he always answered her back. That was one of the things I liked most about him. Out of all the people in our class, he was the least scared of her.

"What makes you think she wants to talk to *you*?" Chloe replied. "If you have anything to say to her, you can say it in front of me." She pulled on my arm. "Go away, Ed. You're so annoying."

She went to grab my arm to steer me away. I started feeling really anxious.

Please don't say anything about swimming, I thought to myself.

"I was wondering if you'd like to come to the cinema with me this weekend?" he blurted out, ignoring Chloe completely. "My mum says she'll drive us there."

Chloe burst out laughing.

"Are you serious?" she said, spluttering. "*You* want to go on a date with Molly?"

"It's not a date," Ed replied, and turned bright red. "We'd only be going as friends."

"Well, you're not friends, so I don't know why you're even asking," Chloe said. "And if she wanted to go on a date, it certainly wouldn't be with *you*. Isn't that right, Molly?"

I didn't know what to say. If Chloe thought I was friends with Ed, she'd disown me forever. I just knew it. Our friendship looked like it was on the up since she'd sat with me earlier, and the last thing I wanted to do was ruin it again.

But, at the same time, Ed was my friend too.

"Molly...?" Ed asked, his eyes widening.

"I wouldn't go to the cinema with you if you were the last boy in the world," I said, the words trickling out of my mouth like venom.

Ed looked crestfallen. Chloe laughed. And I felt *dreadful*.

He looked hurt, but didn't say anything in response. Instead he just turned round and walked away.

"What a loser," Chloe said.

But if anyone felt like a loser, it was me.

We got our lunch and sat down with Neada and Jess. I felt absolutely terrible. I couldn't believe I'd said something so horrible to my friend. It wasn't even true! How could I possibly face Ed at swimming again?

I began wolfing my food down. I couldn't stop.

"God, do you ever stop eating?" Chloe asked me, and sniggered to herself.

"*Chloe*," Jess hissed.

"What?" she replied. "She doesn't stop. She's like a pig, gobbling food down like there's no tomorrow. *Gobble, gobble, gobble*. It's so embarrassing."

The shame I'd felt at Chloe's birthday suddenly returned, stronger than ever. Chloe knew I wouldn't say anything back to her. I flushed bright red and glanced at my plate, looking guiltily at the lumps of mashed potato glistening in gravy.

"I'm trying to do you a favour," Chloe said to me. "Stop being so sensitive, Molly. All I'm saying is that you need to stop eating so much. Do you want to be popular, or do you want to be just another fat Gabby-no-friends-Morris?"

"Chloe..." Neada said, and glanced above Chloe's head.

"What?" Chloe snapped at her.

We looked up. Gabby Morris was standing right behind Chloe and had heard every word she'd said.

"I may be fat, Chloe," she said, clutching her tray, "but at least I'll never be a horrible person like you."

10

Ed wouldn't look at me in the car when Mr Davidson picked me up the next morning. He barely opened his mouth the entire journey, except for a few grunts or murmurs, and spent the majority of the time staring out of the car window.

"You're awfully quiet today, Ed," said Mr Davidson. "Everything all right?"

But Ed didn't say a thing.

He didn't talk to me during swimming class.

He didn't talk to me at breakfast club.

He didn't speak to me in school.

And it was all my fault.

I tried approaching him in class when Chloe went to the loo, but he looked at the whiteboard and pretended I wasn't there, blocking out anything I was saying to him. At swimming practice on Wednesday night I tried talking to him in the pool, but he swam away. I'd completely ruined our friendship and I didn't know what to do to make it better again.

I wanted to tell Nan about what happened with Ed, but I knew she'd be so disappointed at what I'd said to him. It still wouldn't be anywhere near the amount of disappointment I felt in myself. I'd glance at him across the classroom, hoping to catch his eye, wondering why I'd been so horrible to someone who had been nothing but kind to me.

Mum was still staying with us in the spare bedroom. Sometimes it felt as though she was a house guest – her overnight bag lay on the carpet for days and her clothes hadn't been taken out and put away properly. I'd often take a peek through the door as I walked past to see whether her things were still in there or not. I was convinced I'd look in there one day to find all her belongings gone.

But a week and a half later Mum was still there. It didn't seem like she was planning on leaving at all. She was really trying to make a good impression with Nan and Grandad and to help around the house in whatever way she could. She'd pick up the food shopping while Nan was at work and tidy up the kitchen and living room. She wasn't a very good cook (she admitted so herself), but she did try making us all fish finger sandwiches one night. Even Grandad seemed to be appreciative of her efforts – though he didn't tell her that, of course.

One night, when she was in the shower, I sneaked inside her room to take a look at her stuff. I wanted to know more about her and the things she liked.

I rooted through her bag and found a leopard-print skirt, an old leather jacket and some posh pink lipstick. I put the leather jacket on my shoulders and swiped the lipstick across my lips, standing in front of the mirror and pretending to pose like the models I saw in Nan's magazines.

I looked ridiculous. I hated my giant legs and arms. Why wasn't I dainty and pretty like the others? My legs alone looked the same size as some of the models' bodies.

Mum, on the other hand, started to look much better. Nan took her for a new haircut and she began to look pretty again. Her cheeks were looking rosier, and the grey around her eyes seemed to fade. She was looking more and more like the photo I had of her in my room. She was looking more and more like my *mum*.

Chloe was making an effort with me too. She'd started being nicer to me since I'd been mean to Ed, as though I'd somehow proven my loyalty towards her. I hate to admit it, but I quite *liked* being in her good books, even if that had meant doing something horrible. It was much better than being on her bad side.

She was being really horrible to everyone else though – a lot more than usual, and that was saying something. She wouldn't hide her disgust towards Gabby Morris, making pig noises as she walked past us in class. She stopped doing her homework and would get in trouble with Mrs Ingram for constantly chatting. She even kept calling Neada "thick" when she got the answers wrong in class.

I started to hear a rumour that the younger kids

in school were scared of her. I couldn't blame them – I often got the impression that some of the teachers were scared of Chloe too.

"You've seemed a bit down the last few days," Mum said on Thursday evening, sitting at the kitchen table and reading a magazine. My arms and legs were aching from that week's swimming practice, and on top of my falling-out with Ed, I wasn't exactly in the best of moods. Nan and Grandad were having a quick nap in the living room, in front of the early-evening news, the light from the telly flickering on the walls. "What have you got to feel so glum about?"

"I fell out with a friend," I said, which wasn't a lie, but wasn't the entire truth either. The *truth* was that I'd been horrible to someone who'd done nothing to deserve it.

"I'm sure you'll work things out," she said, putting her arm round my shoulders.

I'd noticed that whenever Mum hugged me or showed me any kind of affection, it always felt a bit forced and unnatural. It felt wrong to say, like I was being disloyal, but it didn't feel warm and homely in the same way Nan was with me.

"Tell you what," she said. "Why don't we go shopping? That always cheers me up when I'm feeling down."

"Now?" I asked, surprised. It was a school night, after all.

"Yes!" she said, a bit too excitedly. "Come on, let's go!"

Nan was fast asleep on the sofa. "Don't disturb her," Mum whispered, and grabbed Nan's car keys from the kitchen. I'd never used shopping as a way to cheer myself up, but it was nice that Mum was making an effort with me. So off we went, leaving Nan and Grandad snoring in the living room and driving to Riverdale, like normal mums do with their daughters.

It was shopping the way I imagined Chloe, Neada and Jess did with their mums – not like with Nan, who'd drag me from one boring shop to another. We walked round Riverdale arm in arm, ogling the expensive jewellery and handbags in the shop windows. We made pretend shopping lists in our heads, imagining all the things we'd buy if we had millions of pounds to spend. We sang loudly to the tunes playing in the shops, making old ladies tut at us. Mum just ignored them and danced in the middle of the shopping centre, making me laugh harder than I had in a long time.

She was *so* much fun – like an older sister without any responsibilities. She was more fun than Chloe's mum, and that was saying something. I couldn't wait for my friends to meet her and see how great she was.

We walked past the shop with the same red dress that Nan wouldn't let me have. I stared at it dreamily, imagining how beautiful and glamorous I'd look wearing it.

Mum must've seen me ogling it.

"Do you like that dress?" she asked.

I nodded. "I tried it on the other day. Nan thinks it's too short or something."

"*Pfft*, what does Nan know?" she said. "*I'm* your mum and *I'll* decide what you can and can't wear."

Mum pulled me by the arm into the shop. I knew Nan would kill me if I came home with it, but the fact I couldn't have it made me want it even more.

"What size are you?"

I picked the size off the rail that had fitted me in the changing room and handed it to her.

"Yeah, that's *gorge*," she said, rubbing the red

starry fabric between her palms and fingers. "I knew my daughter would have good taste. You take after me."

Without saying a word, Mum took it to the checkout and paid for it. I couldn't believe it – first a phone and now my dream dress!

"Thanks, Mum!" I said, bursting with excitement as she handed me the shopping bag. It was the best present in the world. Chloe was going to be so jealous when she saw it.

"Don't you worry, my darling," she replied. "Now, how about we go for something to eat?"

"It'll be dinner time soon though," I said, thinking of the time. It was starting to get late. "I know Nan's got a chicken ready for us in the fridge."

"Oh, come on," she said. "Why do you have to be so boring all the time? I fancy a burger."

We climbed up the escalator to the food hall. I ordered a cheeseburger with a big portion of chips and lemonade. Mum ordered a burger with chips and a Diet Coke. She told me she was watching what she was eating, which I thought was so silly, as she was as thin as a rake. From the corner of my eye I saw her reach into her bag and pull out a hip flask, pouring out whatever contents were left inside it into her drink underneath the table.

"What's that?" I asked curiously.

"Just something to make it taste better," she said quickly, and shoved the flask back into her handbag like she had something to hide. "Coke tastes a bit funny on its own, don't you think?"

I was worried that I wouldn't be able to eat dinner once we got home, especially after eating such a heavy meal, but it must've been all right to eat at that time if Mum said it was. She *was* the grown-up, after all.

I was having a great time. I never knew mums could be this much fun. We laughed and laughed at the table over the silliest of things, like when we saw an old man snoring on a bench on his own.

But there was a part of me that felt anxious too. I really didn't want Nan to worry about where we were and I knew what she was like. Nan worries about everything, like if I pop to the newsagent's on my own and stay looking at the magazines and sweets too long. But I couldn't ring her myself to tell her I was all right because I'd left my new phone at home.

"So, talk to me about boys," she said, sipping her Coke slowly through a straw. "Anyone you fancy?"

She'd clearly forgotten that she'd already asked me that question when we'd spoken on the phone. Sometimes it felt as if she never listened to what I said. She never seemed interested in knowing how school was going or what tests I'd passed – just what boys I had a crush on. What was so great about having a boyfriend anyway?

This time, however – and I didn't know why – all I could think about was Ed. His face and silly expressions kept flipping through my mind like a pack of cards and my tummy felt like it was doing backflips. It must've been the guilt setting in again.

"No," I replied. "I have – well, *had* – a best boy friend called Ed who I go swimming with, but he doesn't fancy me."

Why did I keep thinking about him?! It was so inappropriate.

"I'm sure he does," Mum replied. "And if he doesn't fancy you, then he must be blind. We've got to dress you up a bit better. Then he'll notice."

"*Mum*," I said, mortified that someone nearby

might've heard.

"Trust me," she said confidently. "I may not be good at everything, but when it comes to men, I know a *lot*."

There was one thing I wanted to know that I hadn't got round to asking Mum about yet. I'd never asked Nan, because speaking about Mum always brought a painful expression to her face, like she was hurting from something. But Mum was in a great mood, and if I knew anything, asking grown-ups for things when they were in a good mood usually meant you could get what you want.

"Who's my dad?" I asked. "Was it that man you drove off with that time?"

Mum put her drink down and looked at me. I suddenly wished I hadn't said anything at all. I had a habit of ruining things.

"Why are you asking me that?" she replied, sounding annoyed.

"Well ... it's just that I just don't know anything about him. I don't even have a picture of him. I don't even know his name."

"It was a mistake," she answered. "A silly mistake I made at sixteen that I wish I could take back, but hey-ho – it's one I won't be making again. I don't know who he is myself. I couldn't even begin to know where to look for him. So best try not thinking about it, eh?"

A mistake? Me? My heart felt shattered. Did that mean Mum didn't really want me at all?

She put her hand on mine from across the table.

"Listen – you've got me, and I've got you," she said dismissively, "and that's all that matters."

And like that, my heart felt mended again.

We arrived home at ten o'clock, almost three and a half hours after we'd left. Even though I'd had the best time with Mum, I knew I was going to be in so much trouble for not letting Nan know where I was.

But weirdly, I wasn't the one Nan yelled at.

"Where have you been!" she screamed at Mum as we walked through the door. "I've been absolutely *frantic*!"

She pulled me into her chest and wrapped her arms around me like she never wanted to let me go, resting her face on top of my head and breathing in my hair. Grandad was standing behind her, clutching so hard on to his walking stick that his knuckles were white.

"What the hell were you playing at, Angela?" he said angrily. "We were about to call the police and file a missing person's report!"

"Thank God you're safe," Nan said to me quietly. I felt Nan was blowing everything out of proportion again, like she always does. At the same time though, it *did* feel quite nice that Nan had missed me that much.

Mum didn't seem to care in the slightest. She folded her arms and slouched against the wall.

"You're acting as though I can't take my own daughter out for the evening," she replied. "We went late-night shopping, for God's sake. I'm perfectly entitled to do that. We were having a nice time."

I felt bad that she was being yelled at by Nan and Grandad. It felt a bit like she was being ganged-up on. Going out without telling Nan wasn't *that* much of a big deal, was it?

"I had a great time, Nan. Honest," I murmured, though perhaps not quite loud enough. I quickly hid the shopping bag with the dream dress behind my back, just so Mum wouldn't get in trouble for that too.

"It's a Thursday night!" Grandad yelled at her. "She has swimming practice tomorrow morning!"

Mum yawned and rolled her eyes. Nan looked as though she wanted to slap her.

"Why don't you go to your room, Molly?" Nan said, forcing a smile and trying to sound like there wasn't a problem. "I'll come upstairs and say goodnight in a minute."

I really didn't want to deal with any more drama. Arguments seemed to follow me wherever I went recently, and I was sick of them. I hurried upstairs and closed my bedroom door, trying to block out the sound of the yelling downstairs.

11

Mum was already awake when I got up early for swimming the next morning. I'd almost expected to find her gone after the racket she'd caused last night. The yelling seemed to go on forever and ever, echoing all the way up the stairs and along the landing, until I'd eventually managed to zone it out and fall asleep.

She was sat at the kitchen table, one hand on her forehead and a cup of coffee in the other. She was dressed in a scruffy pink dressing gown that looked older than I was and her hair was tied up in a bun.

Grandad was also sat at the table, munching on some toast and reading the paper. Apart from the rustling of the newspaper, they were both sitting in complete silence, avoiding any kind of eye contact.

"Ready for swimming?" Grandad asked, glancing up at me as I walked in the room. "Let me make you some breakfast."

"I'll do it," Mum offered, getting out of her seat.

"It's fine, Angela," he replied sternly, and Mum sat back down. He turned to look at me. "Eggs OK?"

I smiled and nodded, trying to pretend that everything was fine. "Yes, please."

He went to the fridge and glanced around inside.

"Hmm, we seem to have run out of them. Let me pop to the larder and see if there's any left in there."

We watched as Grandad hobbled out of the kitchen. He still looked frail. Mum sipped a bit more coffee, then turned to look at me.

"I seem to be making a grand mess of things, don't I, Mol?" she said sadly. "I'd been on my best behaviour up until last night and now I've ruined it again. I just wanted us to have some fun, that was all."

"I know you did," I replied, and I put my arm round her shoulders the way I see grown-ups do whenever there's a crisis.

"I really shouldn't have spoken to your nan and grandad like that," she said. "I shouldn't have taken you out in the state I was in either. I feel really bad about it. I'll make it up to you all, I promise. Promise, promise, *promise*."

Nan suddenly appeared in the doorway, also in her dressing gown. It wasn't like her to be up this early.

"Morning," she said, not very cheerily. She glanced at Mum and then at me.

"I'm really sorry about last night," Mum said quickly. She did seem genuinely sorry for whatever it was that Nan was unhappy about.

"It's fine, Angela."

"No, I really am. I mean, I'd had a bit too much—" Mum started, before Nan put her hand up to tell her to be quiet.

"Not now. Not in front of Molly. It's *fine*."

I didn't understand why Nan was being so harsh with her, or why – once AGAIN – I was being

86

treated like a child that needed to be left out of things. Mum had apologised, after all. Wasn't that enough?

"Have you got your swimming things ready?" Nan asked me, changing the subject entirely.

I nodded.

"Oh yeah – *swimming*!" Mum said a bit too enthusiastically. I could see she was trying her best to be chatty and to make an effort with us. "When's your competition again?"

"In four weeks," I replied, and my stomach began churning into knots. I didn't have much time left to practise and although Mr Davidson kept telling me I was more than ready to compete, I still felt I had a long way to go.

I didn't want to let anyone down. I wanted to show everyone how great I was. I *needed* to win.

"I can't wait to come and watch you," she said.

My heart skipped a beat. She'd never been to anything I'd taken part in before, although I'd always look out for her and try to spot her in the crowd. Hearing her say those few words made me feel like my life was whole. If in that moment my entire body could've beamed with happiness, you would've seen it shine from space.

"Are you definitely going to come?" I asked excitedly. "Really? Honestly, I'm going to swim my absolute *best* for you, Mum. Just you wait."

"Drink your tea, Molly," Nan said before Mum could reply, and I fell back down to earth with a bump.

I got into Mr Davidson's beaten-up car, staring back at the house and praying that Mum would still be at home when I got back. I hoped Nan and Grandad wouldn't be too harsh on her.

Ed ignored me, of course. We drove off and I let out a huge sigh, staring out of the window and watching the houses fly past us in a long beige blur.

"Right," Mr Davidson said about five minutes down the road. "I've had enough of this."

Rather than driving the usual way, he took a left turn and went down a different street.

"This isn't the way to the leisure centre," Ed said, confused. It was the first thing I'd heard him say for a while.

"I know it's not," Mr Davidson said, and pulled into a parking space on the side of the road. He turned the engine off and turned round in his seat to stare at us.

"What is wrong with you two?" he asked. "And don't say 'nothing', because you've completely ignored each other the last couple of weeks. There's something going on and I want it sorted. I thought you were meant to be friends?"

"So did I," Ed muttered.

"Come on, you two," said Mr Davidson. "Let's sort this out. You're a team. You can't ignore each other forever. Life's too short to fall out over petty things."

"It wasn't petty to me," Ed said.

It was clear that Ed was still hurting a lot from what I'd said to him in front of Chloe. I just wish we could've sorted it out between just us, rather than in a car with a teacher.

"Anything you have to say to Ed, Molly?" Mr Davidson asked.

I knew that he knew I was to blame for all of this. I could've apologised there and then for what I'd said to Ed in front of Chloe – apologised for being so cruel and unkind to him. But admitting what I'd said to Ed in front of Mr Davidson felt too shameful.

"*No*," I answered quietly. I glanced down into

my lap, hoping the conversation would end there and then.

"Very well then," Mr Davidson said, and we drove off to the leisure centre without so much as another word.

"Now, have you all got your zoo money?" Mrs Ingram asked everyone when we arrived in class later that morning. Our school always arranges a leaving trip for the Year 6s, and the zoo was what we had voted on.

"Oh God, I completely forgot to bring the money with me," Neada said, hitting herself on the forehead with her palm. "I'm so forgetful."

Chloe rolled her eyes at Jess.

"Of course she did," she said, and sniggered.

"I did as well," I said, trying to ignore Chloe. "Sorry, Mrs Ingram."

The truth was, I hadn't mentioned our zoo trip to Nan, or even bothered handing Mrs Ingram's letter about it to her. I *knew* she'd probably moan about how the school was trying to take her money again, or go on about how *her* mum had never been expected to fork out for day trips when she was at school. She'd always say the same thing:

90

"I'm not made of money, Molly."

I didn't want to miss out on the trip, of course, but at the same time I didn't know how I could ask Nan about it. Money was always such an awkward topic at home. I knew we didn't have much of it.

"You have until tomorrow morning to get the money to me, you two," she said to us. "The trip's on Monday. You don't want to miss out, do you?"

Neada shook her head. I wasn't sure if I cared or not.

Jess and Chloe handed her their envelopes of cash. It was easy for them – their parents gave them whatever money they needed.

"Miss, are we allowed to wear normal clothes?" Chloe asked. "I don't want to be stuck wearing this ugly uniform on a school trip when we're supposed to be having fun."

"Well, I was assuming you would all wear your uniforms…" she began to answer.

"*Noooooooo!*" came a groan of voices from around the room. I kept quiet, hoping Mrs Ingram would hold her ground and stick to the original plan.

"Oh, go on then," Mrs Ingram said. "I suppose

it won't cause any harm."

Everyone cheered. I sat in silence.

"You better find something good to wear," Chloe whispered to me with a smirk, as Mrs Ingram turned her back to us.

Great. Now I had to find something nice to wear to impress Chloe, as well as convincing Nan to give me the money for the school trip. Was the outfit Nan had bought me from Riverdale worthy of her standards? The day was turning into a hugely stressful one.

I glanced across the room at Ed. I could've sworn I'd caught him looking at me, but his head swivelled to the front of the class before I managed to make eye contact with him. I just wish he knew how desperate I was for us to be friends again.

Nan picked me up from school that afternoon.

"How was work?" I asked as cheerily as I could muster, climbing into the passenger seat and giving her a kiss on her cheek. I knew I had to be nice to her in order to get the money for the trip so I figured I should start as soon as possible.

"Do you not want to talk about last night?" Nan

asked, raising an eyebrow.

I'd tried my best to clear the argument out of my head, so I wasn't entirely sure why she was bringing it up again.

"Did you ask Mum to leave?" I asked.

"No," she said. She paused for a bit. "Most people would have done after the way she behaved, but no. I didn't."

I felt a huge sense of relief. Part of me was expecting Mum to have been kicked out by the time I got home. I'd been trying to prepare myself for it all day just in case. I knew not to get my hopes up about Mum sticking around.

"Look," she said. "I know you don't want to have this conversation, Molly, but it needs to be said. I *know* she's my daughter, and I love her dearly, but I don't want you to depend on your mum too much."

"What do you mean?" I asked, offended that she'd say such a thing. I felt Nan had done nothing but pick on Mum since she'd arrived and it was really getting on my nerves. "She's trying really hard to be a great mum, and you're not giving her a chance. She's buying me loads of presents and everything."

Nan looked ahead at the road.

"Hmmm," she murmured, which wasn't very helpful.

She was being so *irritating*.

"I don't understand why you're getting so annoyed about her driving me to Riverdale," I said. "You're overreacting, just like you always do."

"It was about more than just taking you out shopping, Molly," Nan said, starting to get annoyed herself. "She wasn't being a responsible adult. She was... Oh, I don't even know why I'm having this conversation with you. You're too young to understand."

That comment annoyed me even more. Why did adults think they could treat me like a baby the whole time? And why wasn't Nan just getting to the point?

"I think you're being really mean to her," I said. "And Grandad is as well. I thought you would've liked the extra help around the house, seeing as Grandad makes me out to be such a *burden* on you both."

"Pardon?" Nan replied. "Whatever made you think that?"

I thought back to the night when Mum first arrived.

"Grandad said to her you'd both taken on a big responsibility when she left."

"You've misunderstood that entirely," Nan said. "You could *never* be a burden to anyone, especially not us. We love you. He meant your mother should *act* like a mother and take care of you as well, rather than behaving like a child herself."

She paused for a bit and took a big breath.

"I know you're my granddaughter, Molly, but I see you as more than that. I see you as one of my own – another daughter. And I just worry about you. I don't want to see you get hurt again."

Why was I defending someone who hadn't been there for me over someone who had? Deep down, I *knew* Nan was looking out for me. I knew that she was right about Mum needing to take better care of me. I just didn't want to admit it. After all, who wants to admit their mum doesn't really want them?

12

As Nan opened the front door, we glanced at one another in confusion. The smell of a roast dinner wafted down the hall and hit us as we stepped inside, the sounds of glass and metal clinking from inside the kitchen.

Mum was pottering about the kitchen in her slippers, oven gloves in hand and hair in rollers. The kitchen table had been prepared as though we were in a posh restaurant, with napkins folded neatly in place. She'd even bought Nan a bouquet of beautiful yellow flowers and placed them in the middle of the table. She could've easily passed as a housewife as she boiled vegetables on the stove. She looked just like the type of mum I read about in books – or at least imagined normal mums to be.

"It won't be done for another half an hour yet," she said, clearly a bit flustered.

Nan and I were still a bit shocked and watched her for a few minutes in complete surprise. I didn't feel quite hungry enough for dinner yet, but I could see how much trouble she'd gone to so I told myself I'd eat it anyway.

Grandad had heard us come in and suddenly appeared behind us in the doorway, holding himself upright with his stick. He glanced at Mum from behind our shoulders, but, unlike us, he looked at her as though she was being a complete nuisance.

"It's too early for dinner," Grandad said. "We don't usually eat for hours."

"*Jack*," Nan hissed and glared at him. She turned to Mum and gave her a half-smile – the type you give when you're still annoyed with someone but they've done something nice to try to make things better again. "I think it was very thoughtful of you. Thank you, Angela."

I could see Mum looking at Grandad for approval, but we all knew she wasn't going to get it. He wandered off to the living room and left the three of us alone, closing the living-room door behind him.

"I'll make us all a cup of tea," Mum said quickly, and began filling the kettle up with water. "Sit down, Mum. You must be tired." She turned to me. "How was school today?"

It was the first time she'd seemed genuinely interested. "It was OK," I said, thinking of how I still hadn't fixed things with Ed and how Chloe was still being a pain. "Oh, and before I forget, I have a school trip to the zoo on Monday that needs paying for."

I rooted through my backpack and pulled out the now crumpled letter that had been sitting in there a while.

"This is dated from May, Molly," Nan said as she read it.

"I forgot to give it to you," I lied.

"Still, fifteen pounds though," Nan said, sighing. "Never mind."

I knew you'd say that, I thought to myself.

"I'll pay for it," Mum offered. "She's my daughter,

after all. It's the least I can do."

I kept thinking how rich Mum must've been to afford all these things. She seemed to have a ton of endless cash to spend. But since arriving, she also spent all her days at home not working. I didn't know where the money was coming from.

"No, it's all right, Angela," Nan said. "But thank you for offering."

Grandad's seat lay empty over dinner, his plate left untouched. We could hear the sound of the telly playing in the background. I thought it was rude and unfair that he was putting a stupid TV show over having dinner us. He missed out on a feast though, so it was his loss.

Although she's not the best cook, Mum's dinner was actually *delicious*. It was hands down the best roast I'd ever had, but I wouldn't ever tell Nan that. We had Yorkshire puddings and chicken, roast potatoes, carrots, broccoli and lashings of gravy. I had two portions, even though I wasn't that hungry.

"That was absolutely delicious," Nan said with a smile on her face. Mum stood up to tidy the table but Nan put her hand up. "No, no, let me.

You sit down."

Mum lay back in her chair and rested her hands on her tummy, tired and stuffed. I was so proud of her for making such an effort. She looked like she was proud of herself too.

"Now that I've got you here, I wanted to ask you both something," she said. Nan was scrubbing the plates in the sink but turned round to listen. "I've been thinking about it today and you can say no if you want, but I really want to throw you a birthday party, Molly."

I was confused. It wasn't my birthday. My birthday had been in February and it was now the beginning of June.

"I know it's not your *real* birthday," she said, as though she'd read my mind. "But I thought I could throw you a massive party to make up for missing it. An *'unbirthday'*. What do you reckon?"

In my head, I wanted to say she should be making up for the *eleven* birthdays she'd missed so far, not just this one, but I kept quiet. I appreciated the fact she was making an effort.

"Hmm, I'm not sure how I feel about a load of kids running about in the house," Nan said, wiping up the crumbs on the dinner table with a cloth.

"We'll have it in the garden," Mum said. "We'll get picnic blankets and loads of food and have some music and invite everyone you know."

I liked the sound of the idea, but I knew one person who would probably try to sabotage it in some way.

"I don't think Chloe would want me inviting *everyone*," I said, making a mental list of all the people she didn't like.

"Well, it's not Chloe's birthday, it's *yours*," she said. "And if she doesn't like who's invited, then she can get lost."

I smiled. I knew Chloe wouldn't mess with me if Mum was about. Suddenly I liked the sound of the party even more.

Mum looked at Nan and put her hands together.

"*Pleaassseeeee?*" she said, in the same way I had done with her at Riverdale. "Come on, Mum. Let me show you I can be responsible. It won't be anything too crazy. I won't let you down, I promise."

Nan looked at her and then over at me.

"Go on, then," she said, sighing, and Mum squealed with excitement.

Mum drove me to school early on the Monday morning. We had to be in the car park by eight thirty, ready to board the coach that would drive us all to the zoo.

Mrs Ingram was by the bus and checking everyone off the register, looking a bit stressed. We were running behind because Mum woke up late, so by the time I got there everyone was already on the bus.

"Here, put some lippy on," Mum said, rooting through her bag and passing me her pink lipstick and a small mirror.

"I'm not allowed to wear make-up to school," I replied. I was getting frustrated at how relaxed she was being when we were embarrassingly late.

"Well, in ten minutes' time you'll be on a school bus outside of school," she said. "And *I'm* your mum and *I* say it's fine."

I did as I was told, even though I didn't think she was right. But in all honesty, I did feel very glamorous after putting on the lipstick, smacking my lips together like I'd seen Mum do in her bedroom mirror. Nan never let me wear make-up, so it felt like a treat.

Mum had helped me get changed into my new

outfit before we left – a mini-skirt, a pink T-shirt with "LOVE" written across it and a denim jacket – and, along with the pink lipstick, I felt the prettiest I ever had. It was so great having a mum who knew about fashion.

Mrs Ingram waved at me to hurry out of the car.

"Have a fun day," Mum said, winking at me. "I'm gonna get working on your party invites."

I stepped out the car and headed towards the coach as fast as I could.

Suddenly I realised how short my skirt was. It kept riding up my legs as I walked, so I tried hoisting it down in an attempt to make it look longer. I saw my classmates' faces press up against the window as I walked on over. Unlike Chloe, I *hated* being on display like this.

"Hurry up, Molly," Mrs Ingram said. She glanced down at my outfit disapprovingly. "It's not a fashion show, but never mind. Get on the bus."

"*Oi, oiiiii!*" yelled some stupid boys as I climbed up the stairs. I went bright red and tried searching for the girls as they wolf-whistled. I spotted Ed near the back. He stared back at me but didn't say a thing.

"Molly! Molly! I saved you a seat!" Neada

yelled, and I sat down next to her as quickly as I could. Chloe eyeballed me as I walked down the aisle, her blonde waves glistening in the morning sunlight. She looked like a supermodel sat next to Jess, who was dressed casually in jeans and a football shirt.

"God, attention-seeking or *what*?" Chloe hissed to Jess, but loud enough so I could hear.

"You look lovely, Mol," Neada said, turning to me. "I've never seen you look so glamorous. I wish I looked as good as you."

"You look *ridiculous*," Chloe snapped, turning round in her seat. "Why are you trying to upstage everyone? And why the hell are you wearing lipstick?"

"*You're* wearing lipstick," I replied, looking at the pink on her lips. Chloe didn't know what to say.

"I've always worn it," she said after a few seconds. "You're just trying to be cool and copy me. Make-up is *my* thing."

"It's no one's 'thing', Chloe," Jess said suddenly. "Molly can wear whatever she likes. I think you look amazing, Mol."

Chloe looked like she wanted to hit me, but I

just smirked back and stuck out my tongue.

We were on the coach for what felt like hours. All the boys were being loud and hyperactive, waving at people in the cars driving past. Mrs Ingram looked like she was going to have a heart attack with all the commotion going on. Chloe sat in silence the entire time, taking selfies on her phone or texting, and ignoring Jess completely.

"Where's your phone?" Chloe asked me. "Or has your mum had to take it back because you're so poor?"

Neada squeezed my hand, as though code for "ignore her". It was nice sitting next to her. I knew she was Jess's best friend but I sometimes wished we could all be a gang of three best friends without Chloe.

Once we arrived, Mrs Ingram told us we needed to be in groups of four. Everyone teamed up with their friends, huddling together and being louder than necessary.

Then I spotted Ed on his own.

"Ed!" I yelled across the tarmac before Chloe could say anything. He looked up at me.

"What are you *doing*?" Chloe hissed at me

angrily.

"He's on his own," I replied.

"So? That's not our problem," Chloe replied. "Let him find someone else to tag along with."

"Oh, that's kind, Molly," Mrs Ingram said, catching me mid-wave. "Hurry up now, Ed. You team up with the girls, sweetheart."

Some of the boys sniggered but I didn't care. I wasn't going to leave Ed on his own. Besides, this was the perfect opportunity to try to talk to him and apologise for everything.

"I'm never going to live this down," Chloe said, and raised her hand to her forehead in a dramatic fashion.

"Oh, be *quiet*," Jess said. "Stop being so dramatic. It's not fair to leave someone on their own. You wouldn't like it, Chloe."

Ed walked over to us awkwardly, brushing the hair out of his eyes. His trainers looked beaten and he was wearing a jumper that looked far too big for him.

"Just so you know, loser, I don't want you here," Chloe snarled, as Mrs Ingram passed some maps of the park around.

"Trust me – I don't want to be here either," Ed

replied.

"Oh, can't we all just get along?" Neada pleaded.

"There's no way I'm hanging round with *him*," Chloe said. "And you're both not either," she said to Jess and Neada. She turned to me. "You and your little boyfriend can hang around together for all I care."

I'd had enough of Chloe by this point. I wasn't going to let Neada and Jess's day be ruined by Chloe's behaviour though, so I decided I would go around with Ed on my own. Jess and Neada looked at me desperately, like they wanted to get rid of her, but they didn't say anything. No one ever does when Chloe acts this way.

As we walked to the entrance, Chloe checked to see if Mrs Ingram had stopped looking, then grabbed Jess and Neada before they had a chance to say anything.

"See you later, losers," she yelled, and pulled them in a different direction towards the lion enclosure.

This was the first time since the canteen incident Ed and I had been alone together. We stood there in silence, not knowing where to look.

I knew I had to be brave and to apologise, just like Mum had with Nan. This was my chance to make things right again. I took a deep breath and hoped for the best.

"Ed—" I began, but he'd spoken at the same time.

"Why do you want to be friends with Chloe?" Ed said. "And why are you always trying so hard to impress her?"

I glanced down at the floor.

"She's my best friend," I replied, though I wasn't convinced she was any more, or had been for a long time.

"Well, she's not a good friend to you. Or to Neada and Jess, for that matter. She's horrible to you all and you don't say anything. *No one* likes her."

I decided I should be as honest with Ed as possible. I hadn't been honest with anyone else about how I'd been feeling recently.

"I'm worried that Chloe won't be my friend when we go to secondary school," I said, and went bright red, partly because I knew I shouldn't care if someone as mean as her stayed my friend or not.

Telling Ed my biggest fear felt like a weight had been lifted from my shoulders.

"That's the honest truth, Ed. I feel like I've got to keep her sweet so that she'll stick around and like me. She's been like a sister to me since my mum left. We've always done *everything* together. And I don't want that to end."

"Sisters don't treat each other the way she treats you," he said. "And you've still got Neada and Jess, so I don't know why you're so worried about not having anyone."

I knew Ed was right, but the idea of not having Chloe around made me feel like a baby whose blanket had been taken away. Chloe may have been a pain, but she was also weirdly a comfort.

"Yes, but Jess and Neada have got each other. Those two have always been best friends in the group, and then Chloe and me."

"She's not a friend!" Ed repeated, getting frustrated. "Can't you see that? She's a bully. A nasty, horrible bully who puts you down the whole time. Friends wouldn't do that."

We sat on a bench together, looking out in front of us. In the distance I could make out signs for the seal enclosure. It made me think about swimming again – how I used to pretend I was a dolphin when I was little, diving under the water without a care in the world.

"Chloe doesn't even know I'm entering the swimming regionals, because she told me being in the swimming club wasn't cool," I admitted. "Coming to swimming practice with you guys has been a complete secret. If she found out, then she'd probably *never* hang around with me again."

"But you *love* swimming," Ed said, confused. "You always have. And you're so good at it. You're easily up there with Alice." He paused for a moment. "I just don't understand why someone like you is so worried about what Chloe thinks about them. She hasn't got any kind of talent, except for being pretty."

I suddenly knew the answer to how I'd been feeling.

"Because, Ed," I said, tears welling up in my eyes, "the last thing I want is to be abandoned again."

Ed put his arm round my shoulder.

"Don't cry," he said, giving me a huge hug. "You're not going to be abandoned. And you'll always have me."

"I'm so, *so* sorry for being so horrible to you in front of her," I said, sniffling. "I didn't even mean it. I promise I won't *ever* let anyone treat you like that again." And as I hugged him back, I meant it with all my heart.

13

"Who the hell has an '*unbirthday*'?" Chloe scoffed as the girls opened my party invitations a couple of days later. I wanted them to be the first in the class to get them, so I handed them out in secret at break time when no one else was watching.

"I think an unbirthday is a really funny idea," Jess said, giggling. "Nice one, Molly. I can't wait to come."

"Me neither," said Neada, giving me a hug. "I love the invitations too. Very artistic."

"My mum made them," I said proudly, glancing at the cards she'd spent the last two days making.

She'd typed out all the party details on the computer, glued them on to the back of some star-shaped cardboard and sprinkled them with silver glitter.

Chloe turned her nose up at them, of course.

"If your mum's as 'rich' as you make out she is, why couldn't she afford better invitations?" she said, waving the invite at me. "Isn't this cardboard from a cereal box? They look so *cheap*."

"I think they look great," Jess replied, not bothering to acknowledge Chloe in the slightest.

I couldn't work out if Chloe was annoyed or jealous at Jess's reaction, but, either way, it was quite funny watching her expression change. Neada and Jess were just not interested in a single thing she had to say, no matter how much she tried to get them to notice her. Her lips curled into a frown at the lack of attention and she folded her arms in a huff.

"Guys, remember when my mum got those really fancy invites that were all laser cut?" Chloe said, but Neada spoke over her before she had the chance to finish.

"It'll be so nice finally meeting your mum, Mol," she said sweetly.

I couldn't wait either. I wanted them to see how much fun and how great my mum was. I *finally* had a mum to show off like the other girls did – one that was adventurous, silly and who had a laugh.

"My mum says I can invite everyone in the class," I told them. I made sure that no one was left out, even the people I didn't talk to very much. If Chloe ever threw big parties, she'd often leave two or three people out deliberately and I didn't like that at all.

"So I suppose that means you're inviting that geek Ed and fat Gabby?" Chloe said with a sneer.

I think she was expecting Neada and Jess to laugh, but they didn't at all.

"Yeah, I am actually," I replied, standing my ground.

She raised her eyebrows and smirked.

"Molly can invite whoever she likes, Chloe," Jess said suddenly. "It's her party, not yours. And if you don't want to come, then *don't*."

Chloe looked taken aback. She wasn't used to people answering her back. I liked the fact Jess stood her ground with her. I just wished I had the confidence to do it more myself.

She kept quiet throughout the rest of the day.

In fact, Chloe kept quiet for most of the *week*. For someone as notoriously as loud as she was, she became incredibly subdued. It wasn't like her to be this silent at all.

Later in the canteen, Neada, Jess and I were having fun playing The Taste Game, where we mixed and matched food to see what tasted the best (or, usually, the most disgusting). We'd write what we'd concocted into a notepad, rating the flavours out of ten.

Neada dunked her chips into chocolate pudding.

"Hmm," she said, munching away. "Salty and sweet. I'd rate it a six."

We burst out laughing. Chloe kept staring at a mark on the table with her arms folded, keeping quiet and not joining in. Even *she* liked playing The Taste Game, so I knew something must've been up.

"Are you gonna eat that?" Jess asked, greedily pointing at Chloe's fish and chips that had barely been touched.

Chloe shook her head. "I'm not hungry," she replied quietly.

"Fair enough," Jess said, and went to dip a bit of battered fish into some custard.

I knew something was wrong. I knew Chloe better than anybody. She was usually the star of the show, making sure all eyes were on her at any given moment. She wasn't being as flamboyant as she usually was.

"Is everything all right?" I asked, as Jess and Neada laughed between themselves.

"Yes, why wouldn't it be?" Chloe snapped.

"You're not being very chatty, that's all," I said.

She glared at me with a face of thunder. "Yeah? Well, maybe it's because you're all so boring and immature," she replied, and with that, stormed out of the room and into the playground.

"I really hope this birthday party won't distract you from your swimming contest," Grandad said that evening as we all sat around the TV. It was nice sitting down together as a family, Nan clutching her tea and Grandad filling out the crossword. "It's only a week before you compete."

"I promise it won't," I said. If anything, planning the party distracted me from worrying about the contest so much. I turned to look at Mum. "You're still going to come and watch me swim though, aren't you, Mum?"

"Yeah, yeah, of course," Mum said, tapping away on her phone. It didn't sound like she was listening to me much at all. She'd been hooked to the phone all evening, barely saying a word to any of us.

"Your arms look a lot stronger," Grandad said, smiling. I smiled back. I loved the fact I could see my muscles strengthening with every class. I felt strong, like some sort of superhero.

It didn't matter that Chloe was still in a mood with me. I'd made friends with Ed again and that was all that mattered. Being friends with him and having my mum back felt like all my Christmases had come at once.

I liked that there was never any drama with Ed. He didn't tell me to change my clothes or to stop speaking to other people. He didn't call me fat, even though he saw me in a swimming costume four times a week. Being with him made me feel relaxed – like I was the happiest girl in the world.

He did seem a bit dubious when I gave him my party invite though.

"Are you sure you want me to come?" he asked

suspiciously. "I know you're worried about Chl—"

I interrupted him. "You're the one person I want to be there the most," I said truthfully. "Please come. I won't ever let Chloe be mean to you again."

"I'm so glad you two are back to your old selves," Alice said in swimming club that week. It was an early-morning session and Ed was doing silly impressions once again, the water rippling as I laughed hysterically.

"You both make a fantastic team," Mr Davidson said.

Ed smiled at me. "I'm glad we're friends again too," he said.

I blushed pink and stared down at the water. *What was wrong with me?!*

Alice was standing on the side of the pool next to Mr Davidson, swimming goggles on top of her head and hands on her hips. She clapped her hands, making everyone take notice.

"Right, everyone!" she yelled, and everyone gathered round in the water. Mr Davidson began unpacking plastic bags from out of his backpack, organising them into two piles on the floor. "Mr

Davidson and I have got you all a little something to say well done for all your hard work."

Mr Davidson began calling us out of the pool one by one. We whispered among each other, wondering what these parcels could be

"Molly!" he yelled, and I climbed out, ready to inspect this mysterious package. He handed me a packet and I studied it, opening the plastic neatly.

It was a swimming costume with my name and the school badge printed on the chest. It looked so professional, like the costumes I'd seen the Olympic swimmers wear on TV.

"We thought you all needed to look the part," he said as he handed out more to the rest of the team. "We've got to look the best there!"

"Now you'll really look the part next week," Alice said, squeezing my shoulders. I smiled, though inside my tummy was doing backflips. Seeing the swimming costume meant the regionals were *really happening*.

"Oh, God!" Mr Davidson said to me and Ed suddenly. "Look at the time! We need to get you back to school for breakfast club!"

I didn't have time to dry my hair. The water soaked

through my school jumper and on to my shoulders like a wet fish, making me feel damp and yucky, and I reeked of chlorine.

"Chloe's definitely going to find out I've been swimming now," I whispered to Ed anxiously as Mr Davidson sped down the road. Nan would've had a heart attack if she'd seen how fast we were driving.

We arrived at breakfast club just as the dinner ladies were packing up the food. By this point I was *starving*. They gave us a couple of slices of cold toast, which was better than nothing, I suppose, and we ate them as quickly as we could before rushing off to class.

Luckily my hair was almost dry by the time we got to the classroom. I sat down in my chair and let out a sigh of relief. We'd made it just in time before Mrs Ingram arrived.

"You're late," Chloe said.

I suddenly noticed my swimming kit by my feet. I'd completely forgotten to put it in my locker. I kicked it quietly under my chair, trying to be as discreet as possible.

Then Chloe began sniffing the air.

"What's that smell?" she asked. "It smells like a

swimming pool in here."

My heart suddenly stopped beating in my chest. My palms felt sweaty.

"D-does it?" I asked, trying to sound as surprised as possible.

"I can't smell anything," Jess said curiously.

Chloe's eyes turned into slits. "It's you, isn't it?" she said.

"What do you mean?"

"You've been swimming. Don't lie, Molly. I can smell it."

"No, she hasn't," a voice said from out of the blue. It was Ed, leaning across the table. "I was at swimming practice. Molly wasn't there."

In that moment he might as well have been my knight in shining armour.

"I wasn't talking to you," Chloe snapped at him. Neada and Jess glanced up, their eyes widening.

"Well, I guess the chlorine smell must be me," he said. "Sorry about that."

I let out a breath of air. Luckily for me, my secret was still safe.

"You are still swimming, aren't you?" Jess whispered to me as Chloe left the table to sharpen her pencils.

I went bright red. I didn't want to hide a secret from her or Neada any more.

"Yes," I whispered back. "But please don't tell Chloe. I can't give it up. It's my most favourite thing to do. You both know that."

"We won't tell a soul!" Neada whispered. "Well done for not listening to what Chloe says." She glanced up to make sure Chloe couldn't hear. "Honestly, going round the zoo with her was the most boring thing in the world. She just kept saying mean things the whole time."

"She's horrible," added Jess. "Neada and I have been talking and we don't want to be Chloe's friend any more. We think she's a bully. Especially to Ed and Gabby."

I felt such a sense of relief. Thank goodness I wasn't the only one fed up with her.

"Let's give her one last chance to make it up to us at my party," I said. I knew Chloe was awful but she wouldn't ruin my day ... would she?

14

To say I was nervous about the party was an understatement. I was terrified that nobody would show up, which had left me feeling sick the entire week.

I wasn't as popular as Chloe. I didn't have a ton of friends other than Neada, Jess and Ed, so I couldn't be too sure anyone would come. Most of all, I was worried it wouldn't be good enough for Chloe's tastes.

After everything that had happened recently, I just wanted it to go smoothly, but the lead-up to the day began feeling more and more stressful.

It didn't help that Chloe was putting pressure on me about it at school.

"Is there gonna be nice food?" she asked. Chloe always had the most expensive food at her parties – plates of posh sandwiches filled with exotic flavours like lobster (that nobody ate) and pretend champagne in fancy glasses (that nobody drank).

"Yeah, my mum said there'll be lots," I said, although in truth I had no idea whether there would be food or not. Mum said she was going to make the whole day a surprise, which didn't exactly help with my nerves. She kept telling me it would be the best party ever, but there was a part of me that wasn't entirely convinced. Mum wasn't exactly known for her reliability.

"Make sure you leave some for the guests then," she said, sniggering at her own "joke". I glanced down into my lap, desperately wishing Chloe wouldn't show up at all.

"You'd better start thinking about what you're going to wear for your party," Nan said on the Wednesday night. The day was fast approaching. "Why don't you wear the skirt and top I got you from Riverdale a few weeks ago?"

"She's already got a dress she can wear," Mum said, interrupting her.

Oh God. I'd completely forgotten about my lovely, special dress, which currently lay crumpled in the shopping bag under my bed. I'd hidden it from Nan in case it caused another row, but I guess the secret was out now.

"What dress?" Nan asked. I gulped.

"I got her the red one she liked," Mum said. "You know, the red one with stars on."

Nan looked annoyed but she didn't argue.

"I'm sure you'll look lovely," Nan said, forcing a smile. "You always do."

"Well, go and get it then," Mum said to me. "Get your nan to iron it for you."

I couldn't explain it, but it almost felt like Mum was *trying* to cause trouble.

Nan looked like she wanted to say something again but she kept quiet. I ran upstairs to collect the dress before she had a chance to argue, and watched her iron the fabric until it looked as good as when I'd brought it home from the shop.

On Saturday morning, the day of the party, Mum

and Nan came into my room singing "Happy Birthday". They'd made thick American-style pancakes, decorated with maple syrup and strawberries, and lit a blue candle on top.

"Make a wish!" Mum said as I blew out my candles. "I'm going to make sure you have the best unbirthday *ever.*"

I tried to muster up a smile, but I still felt sick at the prospect of nobody showing up.

"Here you go," Nan said, handing me a present wrapped in metallic pink paper. "This is from both your mum and me."

I unwrapped it slowly, trying to savour the moment as much as I could. Mum looked like she was getting frustrated at how slow I was being.

"Come on, Mol, open it!" she said impatiently. "We haven't got all day."

I tore open the paper. Inside was a make-up kit full of eyeshadow, lip gloss and glitter. It was the same make-up kit I'd seen at Chloe's house a while ago, which she told me had been really expensive, and which she wouldn't let me try.

"*Wow!*" I said, genuinely surprised. I moved my fingers across the plastic casing, wriggling the case so that the make-up glistened in the light.

Aside from the dress, it was the most grown-up thing I owned.

Then I remembered something. "I thought I wasn't allowed to wear make-up?" I asked, looking at Nan, confused.

"Well, it is your unbirthday," Nan said. "You deserve a treat for all the hard work you've put into swimming. And besides, you're getting older now. A little bit of make-up at the weekends won't do any harm."

I leaned across the bed and hugged her tight, giving her a kiss on the cheek.

"Thanks, Nan."

"Right, time to get out of bed," Mum said quickly. "People will be arriving at one and we've got to make you look the star of the show."

I sat in Nan's bedroom at her dressing table, my new make-up kit at my side. Nan began brushing my hair until the curls turned into waves and Mum sat down on the floor to start painting my nails. I felt like some sort of celebrity, being pampered by my lovely assistants.

When I finally got round to putting on my dress, Mum made me do a grand entrance for everyone.

She, Nan and Grandad stood at the foot of the stairs, waiting for me to appear at the top.

"*Ta-dah!*" I yelled, waving my arms in the air. They looked at me in amazement.

"Oh, Molly," Grandad said. "You look so grown up."

"You look beautiful," Nan added.

"That's my girl," Mum said. For the first time ever, she actually sounded *proud* of me. "Right, come downstairs and cover your eyes. I'm done with the garden now."

"No peeking!" Mum said, leading us slowly out into the back garden, my hands in front my eyes. I was too scared to peek anyway. I didn't want to have to pretend to be pleased with something if I wasn't.

"And ... *open!*" she yelled.

Nan and I removed our hands slowly and let out a gasp.

The garden looked like a wonderland. She'd decorated the whole thing to match my red starry dress, which explained the star-shaped invites. There were fairy lights and rows of bunting hanging delicately from the fence and the trees, with music playing across the garden. She'd made lots of different-flavoured sandwiches, and had even managed to find red cups, plates and napkins with silver stars on. She'd found a star-shaped piñata and hung it from a branch, and scattered blankets across the grass for us all to sit on.

There were mini sausages, Scotch eggs, crisps and star-shaped sweets in red bowls, and bottles of cherryade, Coke and lemonade at the end of the table.

"Angela!" gasped Nan, bringing her hands to her face. "This looks *incredible!*"

The food table wasn't the best bit. She'd hired a giant tent and filled it with pillows, blankets and more fairy lights. She'd somehow managed to fit a TV and DVD player in there, with a stack of films nearby for us to watch. It reminded me of Aladdin's cave, conjured up by the work of a magical genie.

"Your grandad helped me sort that," she told me, pointing at the TV. I looked at Grandad, who gave me a nod and smiled. It meant a lot to me that he'd helped her with it.

Mum beamed, clearly pleased with her efforts.

Nan said she was so touched she could cry.

It was nice to see them all getting along. Most of all, it was nice to pretend we were a normal family for once.

"Thank you, Mum," I said, and gave her the biggest hug I possibly could.

"All right, calm down, you'll ruin my dress," she said, though she didn't seem to mind too much at all.

Neada and Jess arrived together first. I'd begged them to come early, just so I had some support in case nobody else showed up. Neada's mum had given Jess a lift, as Jess's mum was taking her brothers to football practice. I don't know Neada's mum very well, but she has black glossy hair like Neada does, and always wears beautiful saris that shimmer when she walks.

"Come and have a look at the garden!" I said, grabbing Neada and Jess by the wrists and leading them down the side of the house to the garden. Neada's mum followed not far behind.

"*Wowwww!*" Neada's mum said. "Who arranged all this?"

"My mum," I said proudly, and pointed to her

across the garden. I watched Mum pouring herself a cup of cherryade at the food table and tapping away at her phone.

"This looks so cool," Neada said in amazement. "And your mum looks so pretty."

"Yeah!" said Jess. "My mum would *never* let me have a party like this."

"I must say, this looks amazing," Neada's mum said, clearly impressed. She glanced over at Mum, who had begun arranging the table again, even though it already looked perfect. "Your mum looks a bit busy right now, Molly, but I'd love to meet her some other time. Say hi to your nan for me."

As she left, Neada and Jess ran over to the food table and began piling up their plates as high as they could.

"You look so pretty, Molly," Neada said in between mouthfuls of crisps, glancing at my dress. I didn't want to seem boastful, but I knew I looked pretty too.

"I bet Chloe's going to be so jealous of you," Jess giggled. "She'd never organise a party as great as this."

Boys and girls from my class began arriving.

Some of them had made a real effort – the boys wearing smart shirts and gel in their hair, and some of the girls wearing party dresses. They "oohed" in amazement at the sparkling lights in the trees and "aahed" in awe at the Aladdin tent.

"This looks great, Mol," a boy called Sam said. Even his friends nodded in agreement. He's head of the school's football team and a lot of the girls in our year fancy him. Neada's never said anything but it's obvious she's started to like him too. I honestly felt like the most popular girl in the world.

Mum went round with food, handing out sausage rolls and sandwiches and making sure everyone was having a good time. Nan was in the kitchen, chatting to some of the parents who had dropped kids off. I didn't understand what I'd been so nervous about. Everything was going fine.

Then Ed arrived, wearing an oversized T-shirt and ripped jeans. I ran over to him and gave him the biggest hug I could – bigger than the one I gave Mum. He was the one person I wanted there the most.

"I'm so glad you could come!" I said, bursting

with excitement. He looked a bit taken aback as I grabbed him, but pleased nonetheless.

"Oh, before I forget! I know it's your unbirthday, but I got you a little something," he said nervously. He began rooting around in the pockets of his jeans. "Well, my mum helped me a bit as I'm useless at buying presents, but I did most of the choosing."

He handed me a small, scruffily-wrapped present and placed it in the palm of my hand. He brushed the hair out of his eyes and looked at me.

"Open it later, not now," he instructed. I put it in my pocket and made a "cross" motion on my heart.

He looked down at my dress. "You look … really lovely, Molly."

I blushed again, trying desperately hard to change the subject somehow.

"Come and get some food!" I said quickly. "There's so much of it."

As I walked over to the table with Ed, Neada had an awkward look on her face.

"Neada ate all the crisps," Jess said, rolling her eyes. Neada was clutching her tummy, an uneasy look on her face.

"I think I ate too many," she said.

"Don't worry," I said, giggling. "I'll go and get some more. We've got plenty left. Wait here, guys."

As I walked across the grass and into the kitchen, I watched Mum go upstairs. I tried to follow her but Nan got in my way before I could leave the room.

"Having a nice time?" she asked. "Everyone seems to be enjoying themselves! We could put a film on in the tent in an hour or so. What do you reckon?"

"Sounds great," I said, filling the bowl up with a mountain of crisps. "Where's Mum got to?"

Suddenly there was a ring at the door. Nan shuffled out of the kitchen to answer it. I'd been having such a fun time that I'd almost forgotten someone was missing.

15

"Hi, Chloe! Hi, Karen!" I heard Nan say as she opened the front door. "Haven't seen you both in a while! How have you been?"

My tummy suddenly felt funny, like I wanted to be sick. I felt *so* nervous that Chloe would try spoiling my party in some way. I walked towards Nan and stood behind her like she was some sort of human shield.

Chloe's mum was standing behind her in the doorway, so I had to pretend I was happy to see her, when deep down I wished she would just vanish. She was dressed in a baby-pink mini dress that had sparkles on it, making her look even more sickly sweet than usual, and her hair fell either side of her face in perfectly plaited pigtails.

"Got a minute, Carol?" Chloe's mum asked. "Could do with a chat."

"Absolutely!" Nan answered. "Fancy a cup of tea? I could do without seeing children for a few moments."

"Go on, Chloe, you run off with Molly," Chloe's mum said, and they wandered into the kitchen together, leaving Chloe and me alone by the doorway.

We glared at each other and folded our arms at the same time.

"Right, let's see what kind of party you've organised," she said slyly, and I felt even more nervous than before, worried whether it would be up to her standards or not.

Without me leading her, Chloe walked round the side of the house and into the middle of the garden. She stood on the grass, hands on her hips, with a mean expression on her face. I could just feel her judging everyone.

I glanced around. Everyone still seemed to be having a fun time, laughing and chatting on the rugs with platefuls of food and hitting the piñata as hard as they could.

She practically death-stared Ed, Neada and Jess, who were all stood laughing and joking together, then turned to look at me.

"This is literally the lamest party I've ever seen," she said. "It's the type of birthday a toddler would have." She marched over to the food table. "I mean, look at this. A garden party is the kind of thing I had when I was *five*."

I went as scarlet as my dress. Was it really as uncool as Chloe said it was? Were the people who said they were enjoying my party just being polite? If anyone knew how to put someone down, it was Chloe.

"All junk food," she tutted. "Then again, I suppose that's all you eat, isn't it? Try not to eat it *all* at once, eh?"

Don't let her get to you, I said to myself.

Neada and Jess spotted Chloe and waved to her from across the garden. She didn't wave back.

"God," Chloe said, hissing to me. "What does Neada look like?"

I thought Neada looked beautiful. She was wearing a beaded turquoise top and jeans, her black glossy hair tied up with a butterfly clip.

"She's got to stop wearing stuff like that if she wants to hang out with us at St Margaret's," she added, rolling her eyes. Then she turned her attention to me. "I see you've started wearing short dresses again. No offence, Mol, but don't your legs look a bit ... well ... *chunky* to be wearing stuff like that?"

I stared at her, gobsmacked. I couldn't believe she was being so nasty and trying to spoil my day.

"I'm going to speak to Neada and Jess," I said, and marched over to them across the grass. I might as well have been wearing my tight-fitting swimming costume, because Chloe made me feel like an enormous whale on show in an aquarium.

I was trying my absolute *best* not to cry, but tears began filling my eyes.

"What's wrong?" Jess asked, putting her hand on my shoulder.

"Was it something Chloe said?" Neada asked.

I nodded. They all turned to look at her from across the garden.

"Just ignore her," Ed said. "She's just jealous because she's not the centre of attention."

"Don't you worry," Jess said. "She isn't going to

ruin your unbirthday. We'll make sure of it."

We had a group hug and Neada wiped the tears from my eyes. I felt a lot brighter again. Jess was right – I didn't need to let Chloe ruin my special day, no matter how mean she was being. Mum had gone to so much effort that I wasn't going to let one spoiled brat ruin it.

"Molly!" I heard a voice say, and we turned to look. Gabby Morris had arrived. She looked beautiful in a pale-blue dress and with a bow in her hair.

"Come and join us, Gabby!" Neada yelled. Gabby looked as though she had won the lottery and hurried over to us, grinning from ear to ear.

Then, all of a sudden, Chloe stuck her leg out. Gabby went flying, landing on the ground in a heap, her beautiful blue dress covered in grass stains.

"*Chloe!*" Jess yelled angrily. "What did you do that for?!"

We ran over to Gabby, who also now had tears in her eyes. I'd never seen Chloe do anything as mean as that. Everyone in the garden turned to stare at Gabby. Her knee was bleeding.

"That was a really nasty thing to do, Chloe,"

Neada said, putting her arm round Gabby's shoulders. "Are you all right, Gabby?"

Gabby sniffed and nodded. I thought she was being very brave.

"Oh, stop being such a baby, Gabby," Chloe said, though I could tell she knew she'd gone too far this time. "It was an accident."

"It definitely *wasn't* an accident," Ed snapped back. "You really are a nasty piece of work, Chloe."

"Oh, shut up, Ed," she answered. "Why have you bothered turning up anyway? Still begging to take Molly out on a date, are we?"

In an instant, I saw red. Chloe had no right speaking to Ed like that, and especially not at my party. I felt heat rise from my toes to the top of my head, like a kettle steaming, and I suddenly exploded.

"Shut up, Chloe!" I yelled angrily. The voice came from the very bottom of my body and echoed around the garden.

"Excuse me?" she answered, sounding surprised and taken aback.

"You heard. Shut up. I'm sick to death of you being so horrible." I could feel my face get hotter as I got angrier. "You think you're so cool but everyone *hates* you. You think you're so popular but no one wants to be your friend."

"W-w-*what*?" Chloe stuttered quietly.

"I have spent *months* trying to impress you," I said. "I've tried buying clothes so you'll like me. I've been horrible to other people so you'll like me. I've even given up my favourite sport just to make you like me." I paused, and then smiled. "Well. So you think."

"What do you mean?"

"I've been swimming in secret," I said. "I've been practising and practising almost every morning to be the best swimmer I can. And guess what – I'm going to enter county regionals and win a medal, whether you like it or not. *No one* will make me give up on my dreams, especially not *you*. And as for Ed and Gabby... You can be as horrible to me as you want, but don't you *dare* be horrible to them. Gabby and Ed have done nothing to you. And yeah, Ed's right – you're a nasty, horrible bully."

The whole party seemed to have gone quiet, except for the sound of music playing in the background. No one knew what to say. But I wasn't done talking.

"And yes, I know I'm bigger than you," I continued. "But I'm not fat. I look great in this dress. And my legs aren't chunky – they're strong and powerful, just like *all* the best swimmers.

"So get lost, Chloe. I know you're just jealous of me. I couldn't care less if you don't want to be my friend. Because I don't ever, ever, *ever* want to be your friend again."

All of a sudden I heard a cheer. Everyone at the party began clapping. Some of the boys started laughing. Chloe looked completely dumbfounded, her eyes as wide as a deer's caught in headlights.

"Go away, Chloe," someone yelled.

"Yeah, Chloe," another voice called. "No one wants you here."

Chloe's eyes began welling up and her cheeks burned bright red. She ran across the garden and through the back door, straight into the kitchen where her mum was still sitting.

Neada, Jess, Gabby and Ed looked at me in shock.

"I can't believe you just did that!" Neada said.

"Me neither!" Jess added. "But doesn't it feel good, Chloe getting a taste of her own medicine?"

16

To be perfectly honest, I didn't know how I felt. I thought getting back at Chloe would make me feel better about myself. Saying what I thought of her made me feel good for a moment, but when I thought back to the words I'd said, it had actually made me feel ... well ... *worse*. Part of me wished I'd just walked away and let her get on with it. Seeing my best friend cry made me feel awful, even if she *had* done it to me countless times before.

"Thank you for sticking up for me," Gabby sniffed, wiping her eyes and nose with the back of her hand.

"Come on, Gabs," Ed said. "Let's get you something to eat." He pulled her up by the hand and across the grass to the food table.

"Molly!" Nan yelled suddenly from the back door. "Can you come here for a minute, please?"

Neada and Jess looked at me nervously. *Great.* I wandered over towards the house, knowing full well I was about to be in big trouble. Perhaps I'd spoken too soon about my party going ahead without any glitches.

"Come and sit down," Nan said calmly, over the sound of Chloe sobbing. I sat down in a spare chair, pretending to be interested in the tablecloth and running my fingers across the gingham design.

When I eventually had the courage to glance up, I noticed Chloe wasn't the only one crying.

Chloe's mum had mascara dripping down her face, making her look a bit like a panda. Her nose was all red and her cheeks looked puffy. She didn't look as pretty as usual. In fact, she actually looked a bit *scary*.

"Chloe's been having a bit of a tough time recently," Nan said softly, putting her hand on my shoulder.

I wanted to yell, "*NO, SHE HASN'T!*" across the table, but thought it best I didn't.

"Chloe's mum and dad are getting divorced," Nan said, and Chloe's mum burst into tears, putting her head into her hands. I wasn't entirely sure where to look. I wasn't used to seeing grown-ups cry.

"He *l-l-left* me!" Chloe's mum stuttered, her cheeks bright red. "For a woman barely older than you girls! She's twenty-two, for God's sake! *Twenty-two!*"

"It's disgusting, Karen," Nan said, as Chloe's mum blew her nose. "You're better off without him."

"I just don't know what I'm going to do," she sobbed. "I gave my life up for him, you know? I don't have any skills or qualifications. I married him so young. I don't know how I'll get a job. And now I'm worried I'll be left with nothing."

I looked over at Chloe. Her eyes were bloodshot. I genuinely felt a bit sorry for her. It kind of made sense now, knowing why she had been so mean. I wouldn't know how to cope if Nan and Grandad broke up.

"I ... I had no idea that was happening, Chloe,"

I said quietly.

She looked very small and fragile in her chair. She was no longer the bolshie character everyone knew her as.

"It's OK," she replied, sniffing quietly. "I didn't want to tell anyone."

I know it didn't excuse Chloe's behaviour, but it *did* explain why she'd been so horrible recently. It's a bit confusing, but Nan once told me that people deal with sadness differently. Some people cry; some don't cry at all. Others lash out and scream at people, and others hide away and become quiet, refusing to talk to anyone.

Then the doorbell rang. Again.

"Who's that *now*?" Nan said, irritated. "I thought all your friends had arrived? Go and answer it, will you, Mol?"

There was a man standing in the entrance, leaning against the door frame. He was the tallest man I'd ever seen, wearing a leather jacket and ripped jeans, with a big itchy beard and grey-blue eyes.

"Is Angela here?" he asked, looking behind me into the house. His voice sounded low and rough, like he'd smoked hundreds of cigarettes.

Unfortunately for me, he smelled like them too.

"Mum!" I yelled up the stairs, not taking my eyes off him. His arms were tanned and covered in green and blue faded tattoos – a lady in a hula skirt and an anchor.

"You must be Milly," he said.

"*Molly*," I replied, although I don't think he was listening.

I heard Mum bounce down the stairs. She appeared behind me, letting out a gasp.

"Matt!" she gasped excitedly. "You made it!"

She pushed past me as if I wasn't there and gave him a huge hug, reaching high on to her tiptoes and throwing her arms round his shoulders. He glanced down at me over her blonde head.

"I've missed you, babe," he said, giving her a kiss on the cheek.

"I wasn't sure you'd show up! Come and see everyone," she said, and brushed past me, leading him by the arm into the kitchen.

"I wouldn't go in there—" I started, but, as usual, Mum didn't listen.

Chloe's mum was still crying in the kitchen, blowing her nose loudly. Nan was rubbing her back, saying "there, there", which didn't seem that helpful in the grand scheme of things.

Nan looked up at Mum as they walked into the room. All of a sudden her face dropped, as though she'd seen a ghost.

"What the hell is he doing here?!" Nan said fiercely.

I'd never heard her sound like that before. She sounded *livid*.

Chloe's mum stopped crying for a second and looked up. We all found ourselves gawping at the big, hairy giant Mum was latched on to. He was so tall, his head almost hit the kitchen ceiling.

"Gosh, look at me, making a huge fool of myself," Chloe's mum said, trying to break the silence and dabbing her eyes with a tissue. "Look at the time, Chloe. We've kept Carol far too long. We should probably leave you all to it."

She stood up and gave Nan a kiss on the cheek, thanking her. Then they scurried out of the kitchen like two little mice, leaving us all staring at one another, not knowing where to look or what to say. Nan was still glaring at Matt angrily.

Chloe glanced over her shoulder as she was leaving, as if she was trying to tell me something. There was a look of guilt and sadness across her face, but I looked away. As much as I felt sorry for her, I was still mad at the things she'd said and how she'd almost ruined my special day.

Nan had a face like thunder. She shut the kitchen door so none of my friends in the garden could hear.

"Jack!" Nan yelled to Grandad, who'd been hiding away in the living room all afternoon. "Get in here!"

Grandad hobbled in a few moments later.

"What's wrong?" he asked, then glanced up at the giant. Like Nan, his face changed suddenly when he saw Matt.

"Dad! You remember—" Mum began, but Grandad interrupted her.

"Remember? Of course I do!" Grandad said angrily. "The guy you decided to run off with and abandon Molly for? How could I possibly forget?"

I didn't know what to say. I felt numb. And then I felt a huge pang of hate filling my body and rushing throughout my veins.

I knew Mum had left with a man when I was little, but I had no idea it had been with this werewolf. Suddenly any anger I felt towards Chloe seemed insignificant. *He* was the reason I never knew my mum properly. *He* was the man who stole my mum away from me. *He* was the man who'd *ruined my life.*

"Nice to see you too, Jack," he said, like he wasn't bothered by Grandad's reaction. I felt my blood boiling.

"It's Molly's birthday, Angela!" Nan said angrily, her voice rising. "Why have you invited him here today of all days?"

"Oh, come on. It's not her *real* birthday," Mum said, rolling her eyes. "You're overreacting once again. And as *I* organised the party, I think *I'm* entitled to invite whoever I want."

I didn't understand why she was being like this. Mum had promised me this was going to be *the* best birthday party to make up for all the others she'd missed. It was like she'd forgotten how special it was supposed to be. She'd made it all about her.

"I want him out," Grandad snapped. "*Now*. What the hell are you playing at, Angela?"

"He's a different person to who he once was," Mum said, moving her body closer towards him protectively. "He's got a proper job now. Haven't you, Matt?"

Matt grunted like an ape.

"Congratulations," Grandad said, though he obviously didn't mean it. "You've finally got a proper job in, what – your late thirties?" He turned to Mum. "You destroyed Molly's life when you ran off with him, abandoning her like that."

"Please stop ruining Molly's day," Nan begged, looking across at everyone. "Please, Matt – just leave."

Mum looked up at Matt and grabbed his hand.

"If he goes, I go," she said defiantly.

We all stared at her in disbelief. I couldn't understand why Mum was being so hurtful. Why was she taking his side? Wasn't I enough? I thought she'd come back for me!

"Then go!" Grandad snapped. "I've truly had enough of you, Angela. You think the whole world revolves around you."

My heart began beating faster and faster. She couldn't go – not now. Not on my unbirthday. Not when we'd started getting to know each other. And not when my swimming contest was just around the corner.

I don't know why I stuck up for her, but the idea of losing her again was too upsetting.

"Please, Grandad," I pleaded, grabbing his arm. "Don't make her leave. Let Matt stay, if that's what Mum wants."

Grandad's eyes widened as he looked down at me. I knew I'd put him in an awkward position. But I also knew he'd take my side.

"Come on, Dad," Mum begged. "Just give him a chance, at least."

And as I looked at Mum, I only wished she cared about me the same way she did Matt.

17

Grandad made Matt sleep in his car that night. I kept peering out of my bedroom window, trying to make sense of the shadows in the dark and making sure he stayed firmly in his car. I could make out the odd wriggling of him lying on the back seat, but I didn't trust him to not break Grandad's rules and come inside.

Matt was allowed to have breakfast with us the next morning. Nan had made us all a fry-up, which *would* have been lovely had Matt not been there.

Then I noticed Ed's present on the kitchen worktop. I must've left it there and forgotten about it as the drama unfolded yesterday. I leaned over and grabbed the box, unwrapping it carefully underneath the table so nobody could see.

It was a ring – a beautiful silver ring in the shape of a dolphin. I put it on my finger and it fit *perfectly*, shining in the morning sun. It was perfect. It wasn't as expensive as a phone but it was better. It was the best present I'd ever, *ever* had.

Nan was trying her best to be polite to Matt but I could tell she wasn't pleased having him there. In my head I nicknamed him "Matt the Prat", because whenever he said anything he sounded incredibly stupid. He also kept referring to Mum as "babe", which got really annoying after a while. Nan's always said she hates the word because it's sexist to women.

"Make us a coffee, will ya, babe?" he asked Mum, chomping on his food noisily. He didn't have any table manners by the looks of things, and didn't eat with his mouth closed, which was *gross*.

Yet Mum happily obliged, running round the kitchen like his slave and fussing over him like a baby. She never fussed over *me* that way.

"So how long do you plan on being around here

for, Matt?" Nan asked, which I knew in grown-up language actually meant "When are you planning on leaving?"

"Dunno," Matt grunted, chewing on a piece of toast. "Depends how long I'm in the area for work, innit."

I hoped he'd leave as soon as possible so that we could just get on with our lives and start becoming a happy family again.

"Ready to go, babe?" he asked Mum. He got up out of his seat – without thanking Nan for breakfast – and threw his coat on.

"Where are you going?" I asked, my heart thumping suddenly. Where were they going? Was she going to run off with him again?

"Oh, we're only off out for a bit of shopping," Mum said. "It's not a big deal, honestly."

"Well, can't Molly go with you?" Nan asked, interrupting.

Mum and Matt looked at one another. I knew they secretly didn't want me tagging along. I knew they wanted to be on their own.

"Oh, it's OK," I said, though it most definitely was *not* OK. "I've got a bit of homework to do actually."

"That's a shame," Matt said, though I could tell by the gleam in his eyes that he was *very* pleased to have Mum to himself.

"Angela, can I have a word?" Nan said, and pulled Mum out of the kitchen by the arm before she had a chance to respond.

Nan must've thought she was speaking quieter than she actually was, because Matt and I could hear everything that was being said through the crack in the door.

"You're her mother," Nan hissed. "So start behaving like it. You can't just leave her out of your plans because Matt's shown up out of the blue."

"But we—" I heard Mum argue, trying to come up with an excuse.

"Imagine how you'd feel in her position. She's your daughter. *She* should be your number-one priority. Not him."

Matt the Prat and I were looking at one another awkwardly, trying to pretend we couldn't hear the conversation happening outside. My eyes turned to slits as I glared at him across the table. I wanted him to know just how much he wasn't welcome here.

"It's ridiculous," Mum said. "I'm trying to spend time with Matt and you're making things awkward for us both. I'm twenty-seven years old and can't have my boyfriend stay in my room with me."

"If you don't like my rules, Angela, you know where the door is."

There was silence for a bit, then they walked back into the kitchen, fake smiles plastered across their faces.

"Are you going to get dressed then?" Mum asked me, trying to sound upbeat. "Come on, you're coming with us."

I really wished Nan hadn't said anything now. The last thing I wanted to do was go shopping with them, especially when I knew I wasn't wanted.

Matt's car was as disgusting as he was. I felt dirty getting into the back seat. It reeked of cigarettes and there was rubbish everywhere – empty crisp packets and chip-shop wrappers on the floor.

He went round to the passenger side and threw the bits of rubbish into the back where I was sitting so Mum didn't have to sit near them. I didn't understand why he couldn't have just thrown the rubbish in the bin that stood right next to the car.

But Mum acted as if he was her knight in shining armour, clearing things out of her way like he would for a princess.

"Watch out," he said, throwing some used coffee cups on the floor by me. One of them hit my knee as it bounced on to the carpet but he didn't apologise.

Nan watched nervously out of the window as we drove off. Matt rolled down the windows and put the radio on full volume, the seats vibrating from the noise.

"Isn't this nice?" Mum yelled over the speakers as we sped down the road. "It's like we're one cute little family!"

I rolled my eyes. I was going to make sure Matt the Prat would *never* become part of my family, if it was the last thing I did.

We drove to the town centre and parked up. Matt got out of the car to pay for the parking. I was embarrassed to be seen with him as he waltzed across the car park in his dirty clothes. He looked like he was in desperate need of a shower.

"He's so lovely, isn't he?" Mum sighed as we watched him walk away.

"*Hmmmm*," I murmured, hoping that made her

aware of how I felt.

She wasn't listening.

"I was thinking," she said, turning to look at me. "Now that we've had some mother–daughter bonding time the last few weeks ... would you like to live with me?"

"With *you*?" I replied.

"Well, don't act so shocked," she said. "I am your mum, after all. I mean, I know I don't have a flat yet or anything. But I will soon, once the council approves my request. They let women with children go to the top of the waiting list, letting them have their own flat, so I told them about you. Isn't that great?"

It didn't feel great at all. It felt like she was deciding things for me, like grown-ups often do.

"We can paint the walls any colour you'd like. And it won't be like at Nan's, with all those stupid rules all the time. We can eat whatever we want, when we want. And we can stay up late every night watching films."

I know it sounds silly but I didn't *want* to spend all night watching films. I liked going to bed early. I liked having a routine.

"But what about Nan and Grandad?" I asked.

I couldn't imagine life without Nan's dinners and hugs. I'd miss Grandad's stories and jokes, even if they weren't *that* funny.

"What about them?" she said, her tone changing.

"Well ... they're a bit like my mum and dad too," I said.

Mum's face suddenly turned sour, like she'd bitten into a very bitter sweet.

"What's that supposed to mean?" she snapped. "They're not your mum and dad at all. *I* am."

"Well, I know you're my *real* mum," I said, starting to feel flustered. "I mean, it's just because I've just lived with them since I was a little baby, and—"

"It sounds like you don't want to live with me at all," Mum replied, and turned to look away. I felt really bad.

"Of course I want to live with you," I said, trying to sound upbeat. "It's just Matt I don't want to live with. Can't we live on our own?"

"Look," she said, sounding annoyed. "I know you don't like him but he's a nice guy, Molly. You don't know him like I do. Give him a chance."

"Well, I don't like him."

"He hasn't done anything for you not to like," she snapped back.

Matt wandered back to the car and opened the door for Mum. She shot me a look as she stepped out, then put on a false smile.

I was annoyed and hurt at what she'd just said. I couldn't believe she'd somehow forgotten they'd driven off and abandoned me as a toddler. I climbed out of the back seat and watched as they giggled and held hands, walking in front of me like I didn't exist.

It was annoying watching Mum and Matt together. Matt would pinch Mum's bum and they'd giggle and kiss each other like teenagers, which was *gross*.

When we got to the town centre Matt suddenly stopped and turned to look at me.

"Now, why don't you be a good girl and let me and your mum have some time alone together?" he said patronisingly. He reached into his pocket and pulled out a crisp ten-pound note, placing it in my hand. "There you go. Walk round the shops and go and treat yourself to something."

"But Nan says I can't go round town by myself," I replied anxiously, looking at Mum for help. Plus, regardless of what Nan said, *I* didn't want to go round town by myself.

Mum looked confused as to whose side to take.

"She *is* a bit young, Matt," Mum said, glancing up at him nervously.

"Oh, come on," Matt said. "She's about to go to secondary school." He widened his eyes and looked at Mum pleadingly.

"I … I suppose it won't do any harm for an hour or so," she replied. She looked down at me. "You'll be all right, won't you, Mol?"

I suppose I didn't have a choice in the matter. I nodded sheepishly, pretending it was all OK. I just wished I'd stayed at home in front of the TV with Nan and Grandad, like we did most Sunday afternoons.

Matt smiled, obviously very pleased with himself, and put his arm round Mum's shoulders.

"See you back here in an hour then," he said, smirking, and off they wandered down the high street together, leaving me standing in the town centre on my own.

I walked around town and peered into the shop windows, but hardly anything was open. There were 'closing down' signs in some shop windows, and old ladies pulling their wheelie shopping bags behind them.

I didn't like being on my own. And I didn't realise how expensive everything was. Ten pounds wasn't going to get me very far at all.

Then I spotted Burgerman, the fast-food place Nan takes me to after school sometimes as a treat. I decided I'd buy myself some lunch. That would help pass the time, surely.

The restaurant wasn't that busy either. I was one of the only people in there, apart from an old man talking to himself and a mum trying to control two rowdy twins. I felt like such a loner sitting on my own.

Then I heard someone call my name.

"Molly!"

I looked up. It was Alice from swimming, carrying some shopping bags. She was dressed in denim shorts and a T-shirt, with make-up on and gold hoops in her ears – completely different to how I was used to seeing her at swimming practice.

"What are you doing here on your own?" she asked. "Where's your mum?"

"She's gone shopping with her boyfriend," I said, trying to sound like it didn't bother me. "I'm allowed to go round by myself, you know. My mum's cool about stuff like that. I have to meet them in an hour."

"Oh," she said. "Well, do you mind if I join you for lunch?"

I shook my head. Alice went up to the cashier, got her burger and chips, then came and sat down next to me. I was happy I had some company.

"So," she said, biting into her burger. "Less than a week to go until the swimming contest. Are you excited?"

"A bit," I said. "But I'm really worried about coming last."

"I'm sure you won't," she replied. "You're easily the best swimmer in the team, Molly."

My eyes lit up. I couldn't believe Alice, the regional champion, thought I was our team's best swimmer!

"And who cares if you do come last?" she added. "The fact you're even competing in such a big competition is what counts."

I knew she was right but that didn't mean I didn't want to win.

"I just really want to make my family proud of me," I admitted. "My grandad is so happy that

I'm entering. I'd love to win a race for him. But I really want to show my mum how great I am at swimming too. She hasn't been around much because she's working away a lot. So it would be great if I could win a medal in front of her."

"The only person you should try to make proud is yourself," she said. "Your family will be proud of you regardless. Trust me."

I wasn't sure Alice was necessarily right there. Whenever I mentioned the swimming contest, Mum had never seemed interested, let alone *proud*. She only seemed proud if I wore something nice or looked pretty.

"Is your mum excited to watch you then?" she asked.

"Yes," I said, swallowing hard on my burger. I hoped that the more confidently I said it, the more likely she was to turn up.

"Well, look," Alice said. "I've got a bit more shopping to do today so I've got to dash off. But keep your head up, Molly. You're going to do amazingly!"

Once Alice left, I popped to a newsagent's, grabbed a Mars bar and went and sat on a bench by the spot Matt told me to wait at. Judging by the wall clock in Burgerman, they should've been there by now, but the high street was practically deserted.

I began fiddling with the ring Ed had bought me. The dolphin twinkled in the sun. It was such a thoughtful present.

After another hour, they still hadn't shown up. My heart had began pounding in my chest, and my hands were feeling sweaty. *Where were they?*

There must've been a reasonable explanation for why they were late. Maybe they got caught up in a shop somewhere. I bet it was all Matt the Prat's fault. *Everything* was his fault.

I had just started munching on my Mars bar when, as though my day couldn't get any worse, I heard a familiar voice.

"Oi, oi!"

My tummy started doing backflips. I couldn't believe it. It was Tom and the Sheep from Chloe's birthday party, walking down the high street towards me in matching blue and black tracksuits. I wished the dolphin on my ring could've sprung to life, batting them away with its fins and carrying me home safely on its back.

I wanted to run away but my body froze. I

couldn't up and leave the spot I'd agreed to meet Mum and Matt at when I knew they'd be arriving back any second. Surely.

"Where's your fit friend?" Tom Beckett asked, swaggering over to me. I was trying my absolute best not to act scared, but it was hard when I was surrounded by six boys on my own.

"I ... I ... don't know," I stuttered, looking for a way to get away.

"Let's be honest, she's probably embarrassed to be seen with you," one of the Sheep joked. "I mean, why would Chloe want to hang around with someone like *you*?"

All those feelings about not being good enough for Chloe bubbled up to the surface again. Besides, I knew what they were saying was true. The boys were only saying what I was thinking.

"Look at you," another said, eyeing me up and down. "You really are a giant pig, aren't you?"

"*Piggy, piggy, piggy,*" Tom sang, which made them laugh even more.

My eyes started to fill with tears and my bottom lip began quivering.

"Should you really be eating that?" another Sheep joked. Before I knew it, he snatched the

Mars bar quickly from out of my hand.

The tears began rolling down my face properly and my cheeks started to burn with shame. I didn't think Tom and the Sheep could've been any nastier than how they'd been at Chloe's birthday, but I suppose I was wrong.

"Let me do you a favour," the same boy joked, and in a matter of seconds, he'd squished the Mars bar on top of my head, twisting it into my hair. The six of them laughed and laughed, their voices echoing around the town centre for what felt like eternity, the caramel gluing the strands of my hair together.

"Oi!" yelled a voice. "You lot! What do you think you're doing! Leave her alone!"

It was Alice, running over to me. "Who the hell do you think you are?" she snarled, putting her arm protectively round my shoulders. "What have you done to her?"

"We were just having a laugh," Tom said. "Weren't we, Molly?"

I was crying properly by this point. Chloe would've thought I was such a baby if she'd seen. The whole experience wasn't a "laugh" to me at all. I was mortified that they'd called me fat again, and even more embarrassed that Mum and Matt had left me waiting around for over an hour.

"Hey – you're that girl from those swimming contests," one of the Sheep noted, eyeing Alice up curiously. "Alice whats-her-face."

Tom raised his eyebrow at us both.

"How do you know each other?" he asked Alice as she wiped the tears from my cheeks.

"If you must know, I've been training Molly for the swimming regionals," she said. "And she's easily the best one on the team."

"Well, that's not true, is it, lads?" Tom said, and the boys began laughing again. "We saw her about a month ago looking like a complete whale on the diving board at the leisure centre."

"Oh, shut up, Tom," Alice snapped angrily. I glanced up, surprised she knew Tom's name. "You know you're only jealous because Molly is good enough for the team and you were too rubbish to get in last year."

The boys started sniggering among themselves again and Tom went bright red.

"*That's not true*," he muttered in embarrassment.

"You know, Tom, no amount of bribing or money from your mum and dad will *ever* get you a place on the swimming team. You're just not good enough. So stop being jealous of someone with more talent than you."

Alice gave him a very rude hand gesture then looked down at me.

"Come on, Molly, we're going," she said, then turned to look at the boys again. "And if I ever see you anywhere near her again, I will punch you all in the face."

Alice led me round the corner and towards her car. I was still crying, though incredibly grateful to her for showing up like my knight in shining armour. Where were Mum and Matt? None of this would've happened if they'd met me at the time they promised.

"Can you contact your mum at all?" Alice said, trying to peel some of the gooey chocolate out of my hair.

"I d-don't have a phone," I sobbed, thinking of the expensive phone she'd bought me that was lying in my bedroom, with a SIM card I couldn't afford to top up. "I really want to go home."

"Then that's where I'm taking you," she said. "You show me the way and we'll get you back."

Nan looked surprised when she answered the door – partly because of the chocolate and caramel smeared on my head, but also because Mum and Matt weren't there.

"What's happened?" she asked nervously, looking between Alice and me quickly.

"I'm Alice, Molly's swimming coach. Molly was in the centre of town on her own and some boys—"

"On her own?" Nan interrupted. "What do you mean? What boys? Where was your mum, Molly?"

I shrugged my shoulders, embarrassed. "Matt gave me ten pounds and told me to go round town on my own," I sniffed. "So I waited for them to show and they didn't come back. Then the boys showed up, and … and…"

"*Jack!*" Nan yelled, and Grandad hobbled out again to see what the commotion was about. He looked as surprised as Nan did when he saw the blubbering, sticky mess I was in. She ushered Alice and me into the living room and sat us both down on the sofa.

I'd never been more grateful to be home.

"Some older boys began picking on Molly," Alice continued. "I think they've been horrible to her before. I caught them cornering her in the street. So I drove her home – I thought that was the best thing to do."

"Yes. Yes, of course it was," Nan said. "Thank you for doing that, Alice. Oh, Molly. Who were these horrible boys?"

I looked down at my lap. The way Nan was speaking, I felt like I was in trouble, or that I'd got Mum into trouble again.

"They're some boys in the year above at St Margaret's," I sniffed again. "And now I'm scared to go there after summer because they'll be there. They called me a whale at Chloe's party. Then today they said I was a pig and that I couldn't swim."

"Well, we all know that's not true," Grandad said, with Alice nodding.

Nan looked devastated, but I could tell she was trying to sound positive.

"Come on. Let's wash that out of your hair," she said. "Thank you for driving her home, Alice. Her mum must've just got caught up somewhere."

I was so spoiled by Nan and Grandad that night. Nan ran me a bath and ordered me a takeaway. I was snuggled up in my pyjamas on the sofa and allowed to watch any programme I wanted on the telly.

But by nine o'clock Mum and Matt still weren't home. They hadn't even rung.

I just felt a soreness in my chest. Mum couldn't have made it more obvious that I wasn't important to her. I needed her so badly in that moment and, once again, she'd abandoned me.

At nine thirty the key turned in the lock. Nan, Grandad and I looked at each other all at once.

Mum rushed into the living room with Matt the Prat trailing not far behind.

"Molly!" she yelled. "Oh, Molly, where have you been?! We've been looking everywhere for you!"

I stared at the TV. I wasn't interested in anything she had to say.

"Why didn't you call?!" Nan yelled. "You really are unbelievable!"

"I didn't want to ring you if I thought I'd lost her!" Mum yelled back. "We've looked everywhere around town for her. Honestly, Molly, I've been so worried."

"Unbelievable," Nan repeated, and rolled her eyes. It looked to me like she had water in them. "Her swimming teacher had to drive her back home. She waited over an hour for you to show up and you didn't."

"Why don't you tell your mum what happened to you while she was waltzing around with her layabout boyfriend?" Grandad asked me. I didn't want to get Mum in trouble, but I wasn't sure I cared any more either. There are only so many times you can stick up for someone who keeps on making mistakes.

"I'll tell you then," Grandad said before I had a chance to reply. "Some older boys picked on her in the middle of the street, calling her a pig and all sorts, and squeezed chocolate into her hair. And had you shown up at the right time, this wouldn't have happened. The poor girl was terrified, for God's sake."

"Well, she shouldn't have run off then," Matt replied. "We told her to wait in a certain spot and she wasn't there when we got there."

I'd never seen Grandad look more furious. Mum tried coming over to me to give me a hug but I flinched. I didn't want her coming near me.

"Oh, for crying out loud," Mum snapped. "The girl's safe, isn't she? Everyone gets bullied once in their lives. This is being blown out of proportion and, as per usual, *I'm* the one in trouble."

There was a deathly silence in the room.

"I think you should leave, Angela," Nan said. "Right now."

"You can't kick me out," Mum said. "I'm your daughter."

Nan looked down at the ground. She didn't need to say anything.

"Fine. If I leave, I'm taking my daughter with me," Mum said.

I looked at Nan in shock. I didn't want to leave. My home was *here*, not with Mum and her stupid boyfriend.

"She's my daughter and I'll decide what's best for her," Mum added, folding her arms defiantly. "Besides, we've already spoken about her living with me, haven't we, Mol?"

Nan looked at me with wide eyes. Mum made it sound like I'd agreed to living with her, which I hadn't.

"What do you mean?" Nan asked. "Don't be so ridiculous. You can't just take her, Angela. I've had her since she was a baby."

"Well, a great job you've done," she replied sarcastically. "Look at the place. It's like a war camp with all these rules and regulations. She's never got anything nice to wear, bless her. It's no wonder the boys picked on her today, is it, really?"

That was it. I knew Nan didn't know a lot about fashion or clothes but she'd always tried her absolute best with me. And I certainly didn't want to leave her.

"I'm staying here with Nan and Grandad," I said firmly. I hated her for what she was doing. "I don't ever, *ever* want to live with you or Matt the Prat."

"What did you just call me?" Matt replied aggressively. "You need to watch your tone."

"You heard her!" Grandad snapped.

"You ungrateful little brat," Mum snarled. "Most kids would *die* to be with their mums."

If only Mum knew how long I'd waited for her to show up throughout my whole life.

If only she knew how many birthdays I waited for her to show up at.

If only she knew how long I would wait for the postman, desperately wishing a letter from her would arrive.

But this was the thing. She didn't.

"MOST MUMS WOULD DIE TO BE WITH THEIR KIDS!" I yelled back at her, the sound bellowing

from my lungs, and off I ran, out of the living room and up the stairs, slamming my bedroom door behind me as loud as I possibly could.

18

Mum and Matt were gone the next morning when I woke up for school.

It was history repeating itself all over again, except this time it hurt more than ever before.

She hadn't left a note or given me a kiss goodbye. She had just disappeared.

All I kept wishing was that I'd never met Mum, or that she'd never come back into my life. She'd caused more harm than good. I began to understand why Nan had told me not to put my faith in her.

In five days' time it was my swimming contest. It

was the one thing I'd wanted Mum to stick around for and, as Nan had predicted, she'd ruined it for me.

I glanced into Mum's bedroom. She'd left a couple of dirty T-shirts lying on top of the cabinet and a few mugs with tea stains round the rim, but other than that it was as though she'd never stayed.

I couldn't believe how much had happened over just a couple of days. What started out as something nice had turned into the worst weekend I'd ever, *ever* had.

When I got to school, my party was the talk of the entire class, though after what had happened yesterday I'd barely had time to think about it. Everyone thought it was amazing how I'd stuck up for myself against Chloe and how she'd run crying into the house.

I suddenly found myself more popular than I'd ever been. People kept saying "hi" to me in class when they'd never said anything to me before. And I knew the only reason why they were interested was because I'd made Chloe cry.

Chloe didn't show up to school that day. Her

mum had called her in "sick", although everyone knew that wasn't the truth. Part of me wished I didn't care that Chloe was upset after how she'd treated everyone for months, but I *did* care. I couldn't help it.

"Is everything OK, Mol?" Neada asked me when Mrs Ingram had her back turned. "You seem awfully quiet."

"I'm fine," I nodded.

It was odd looking at Chloe's empty seat. There had been a time where I would've told her about the arguments I'd had at home, and now I felt I had no one to discuss it with.

"Your party was so great," Jess whispered. "Everyone's talking about it!"

Neada grabbed my hand suddenly. "That's a beautiful ring!" she said, moving it so the dolphin swooped up and down like it was gliding through water. "Who gave it to you?"

I nodded my head towards Ed, who was busy writing in the corner, his tongue out in concentration.

"Oh, Molly!" Neada squealed. "Is he your boyfriend now?"

"You've got a *boyfriend*!" Jess squealed back.

"How exciting is this! Imagine what the girls at St Margaret's will think!"

"No, no..." I began, but they were too busy muttering between themselves to listen. The thought of going to St Margaret's when Tom and the Sheep would be there made me feel physically sick.

As the day went on, my hurt turned into anger.

I missed Chloe. I missed her showing off and being loud in class. I missed Mum. I hated the thought of going home and her not being there. I hated the row we had and I hated the fact she chose Matt the Prat over me.

Gabby Morris and Ed sat with us at lunchtime. Without Chloe there saying mean things, it turned into the friendliest lunch we'd had in a long time, but I still had a bunch of thoughts in my head that wouldn't go away. Tom and the Sheep's comments about my weight were repeating themselves like a broken record.

Piggy, piggy, piggy.

My head felt like a cage full of moths trying desperately to bang their way out. The same pictures kept replaying in my head – Chloe crying,

Nan crying, Grandad yelling, Mum yelling, Tom and the Sheep picking on me and calling me fat.

They were right, I *was* a piggy. *Piggy, piggy, piggy.*

No matter how hard I tried to join in the conversation with the others, the thoughts and mean words just wouldn't disappear.

"You must be nervous about swimming," Jess said as I stared into the distance. "Ed told us it's this weekend. Neada and I will get our mums to drop us off and watch!"

That afternoon, as Mrs Ingram was banging on about maths and how important it was in life, there was a knock on the door.

"Oh, Mr Davidson!" Mrs Ingram said. "What a nice surprise."

"Sorry to interrupt," he said, "but I've got a big announcement to make."

Everyone stopped and looked up.

"Now, as some of you may or may not know, Ed and Molly will be competing in the swimming regionals this Saturday!" he said cheerily. "They've trained so hard for months on end and it would be great if some of you could turn up and show your support."

"Well, isn't that just *wonderful*?" Mrs Ingram said, putting her hands together. "What an amazing achievement."

I looked over at Ed, who, like me, had also turned bright red.

The thought of not having Mum and Chloe there to support me became overwhelming in my head. My heart began thumping and my eyes began filling with tears again.

"Why don't we give them a big round of appl—" Mr Davidson said, but before he finished, the words just fell out of my mouth.

"I'm not going," I said, loudly and abruptly.

Mr Davidson looked at me. In fact, the whole class turned to look at me.

"What do you mean?" Mr Davidson said, laughing nervously as people turned to stare. Neada and Jess looked taken aback and confused.

"I said I'm not going!" I replied. I stood up. "I'm sick of this stupid swimming contest. I didn't even want to do it anyway!"

"You know that's not true," Mr Davidson said. "Sit back down, Molly."

"Just leave me alone!" I yelled. "All of you, just *leave me alone*!"

I ran out the classroom as fast as I could, my shoes squeaking on the corridor floor. I ran and ran until I reached the school entrance, then flung the doors open for breath.

Everything I'd been feeling came to the surface and I began wailing. I'd never cried so much before. I didn't know I had that many tears inside me to cry out.

Mrs Ingram and Mr Davidson appeared not long after. Mrs Ingram was panting as if she'd never run before in her life.

"What on earth is going on with you?" she said in between breaths.

"I could ask you the same question!" Mr Davidson said.

I couldn't hold it in much longer.

"Everything!" I sobbed. "*Everything* is wrong."

"Well, tell us," Mrs Ingram said.

"I've had the worst weekend *ever*," I replied, wiping my eyes. "I really can't compete. There's just no point. I can't do it."

"Now, you listen to me," Mr Davidson said, kneeling down so he was on my level. "There's no such thing as 'can't'." He looked me in the eye. "You're the best swimmer on the team,

Mol. Why would you want to waste such a great opportunity?"

"The two people I want there the most won't show up," I sniffed. "My mum's left me once again. And I had a falling-out with Chloe and made her cry, so she won't show up either."

Mr Davidson and Mrs Ingram looked at one another.

"Chloe's got a few problems at home," Mrs Ingram said. "I know she's been difficult recently – everyone's picked up on it. But you do know you'll make up with her eventually, don't you?"

No matter how hard I tried to think positively, I wasn't sure we ever would.

"I really don't want to be seen in my swimming costume again. Not in front of hundreds of people. I'm *sick* of being made fun of for my weight."

"You think you're *fat*?" Mrs Ingram said. "You? You're strong, Molly. You're a swimmer. You look like all the Olympic swimmers you see on TV. What's wrong with that body shape?"

"If you're going to let two people not turning up ruin a fantastic opportunity for you, then you're not the Molly I thought you were," Mr Davidson said. "Look at the friends you've got back in there who *will* show up. Ed would be devastated if you didn't compete. And so would the rest of the team."

He paused, then put his hand on my shoulder.

"You're a really special girl, Molly. Don't let anyone make you think otherwise."

19

On Monday night Mr Davidson had rung Nan and Grandad and told them what had happened.

I was now the talk of the school for other reasons. People thought I was crazy for running out of the classroom and for yelling at a teacher. Some people said I was a rebel, which couldn't have been further from the truth, really. But I suppose being called rebellious was better than being a laughing stock. I didn't want to be known as a whale any more, or for being Chloe's ugly friend. I wanted to disappear from people's view and never come back.

No matter how much Mr Davidson tried to convince me, by Thursday I still hadn't changed my mind. Neada and Jess weren't sure what to say to me. Ed seemed sad, and I knew it was because I was letting him down. But if Tom and the Sheep thought I looked like a pig, then why wouldn't he?

I hated the fact that I was bigger than Neada, Jess and Chloe. I hated being the odd one out in the group.

I refused to go to the early-morning swimming lessons. Instead, Nan drove me to school at the usual time like everyone else. Eventually, I thought, I wouldn't have this pressure about the swimming contest and could blend into school like all the other girls did.

Nan was getting angrier with me every day for being stubborn, but I didn't care.

"Why are you letting your mum and some stupid boys get the better of you?" she asked.

But no matter what she said, I stayed quiet.

Grandad was awfully quiet too. He barely spoke to me, and if he did, it felt forced – like he was trying to say something else but couldn't quite get it out. I knew I was hurting him by not competing, and I felt bad for letting him down. But I also knew that, like most things, he'd get over it.

Chloe hadn't shown up for school that week at all. Nan tried ringing her mum to see how they were doing but they never called her back. Mr Davidson spotted me in the school corridor and walked the other way. I felt miserable, and I wanted this stupid swimming contest to be over so that I never had to think about it again.

Nan tried to get me out of bed on Saturday morning. She was still acting funny with me and shook my duvet a bit more roughly than usual.

I glanced over at the clock on my bedside table. In less than an hour and a half I was meant to be at the swimming contest I'd trained so hard for.

I glanced up at the ceiling and sighed loudly. Just one more day and this would all be over. I rolled out of bed and downstairs to the kitchen, pouring myself a bowl of Coco Pops. Grandad was in the living room watching the early-morning cooking shows, and Nan was upstairs in her room.

I couldn't put my finger on it, but the house felt strange and unhappy, like someone had died in it. I just wanted things to go back to how they were before Mum had ruined it for us.

I began wondering where she and Matt were. I pictured Matt squeezing her bum again (yuck!) and her laughing hysterically at his seriously unfunny jokes. I bet they'd moved into their new flat by now and painted the walls the colours she wanted. I bet they were both so happy that I wasn't there to spoil their fun.

Ed's dolphin ring clinked against my spoon. I bet he was at the swimming contest already with the others. I pictured the team having fun together and Ed making them all laugh. They'd all be standing round wearing their costumes with pride by now. And yet here I was, sitting in the kitchen on my own.

As I glanced down to look at the ring in more detail, the silver twinkling in the morning sunlight, I began thinking of the words Mr Davidson had said to me.

If you're going to let two people not turning up ruin a fantastic opportunity for you, then you're not the Molly I thought you were.

You're a really special girl, Molly. Don't ever forget that.

Don't let anyone make you think otherwise.

For God's sake! Why was I worried about what

Mum was doing? Why was I going to let someone who didn't care enough about me ruin my big day? And why did I care if she didn't show up, when all the people in my life that cared about me the most were going to be there?

This was *my* chance to shine.

I wasn't going to let anyone down. And I certainly wasn't going to let anyone else ruin it.

I sprang off my seat and quickly ran upstairs, opening my cabinet drawer and pulling out the special swimming costume that Alice and Mr Davidson had given me. I pulled the Lycra over my strong legs and over my squishy tummy, adjusting the straps over and under my muscly arms.

I glanced at myself in the mirror. I looked strong and powerful. Tom and his gang of Sheep didn't know what they were talking about. Alice was right. I was the one who made the team. Not him.

I grabbed my goggles and swimming kit and rushed to the top of the stairs, pulling my tracksuit bottoms on as quickly as I could.

"NAN! GRANDAD!" I yelled as loudly as I could. "Get me to the swimming contest! We haven't got much time!"

We bundled ourselves into the car – Grandad,

Nan and me. We'd never been to this swimming centre before, so finding the address on the satnav was taking more time than expected.

"Hurry up!" Nan said to Grandad.

"I'm trying!" he said.

Nan pulled out of the driveway and we sped down the road, faster than Nan had ever driven before. No one needed to say anything, but I could tell my stubbornness was forgiven.

The wheels of the car screeched as we pulled into the swimming centre. Nan drove around trying to find a parking spot. The car park was full of other kids from other teams, all wearing their different school colours.

Grandad couldn't run, obviously, but Nan and I did. He told us he'd meet us in there. I rushed through the leisure centre doors and to the main pool area, trying desperately hard to find my teammates among the crowd of people from other schools.

Then I spotted Alice's tall frame in the crowd.

"Molly!" Alice yelled, spotting me, and everyone in the team turned to look. I spotted Ed and Mr Davidson, whose faces turned into large grins.

"I'm so sorry I'm late," I said, pulling my tracksuit bottoms off and flinging them on the floor. I looked at Mr Davidson. "I'm sor—"

"You're here," Mr Davidson said. "That's all that matters. Give us your stuff and get to the side of the pool. You're almost ready to go."

Alice grabbed my belongings from me and started leading me to the side of the pool. I saw Nan and Grandad find their places in the audience. By this point almost all the seats were taken.

Best of all, Neada, Jess and Gabby Morris were sitting there too. Neada nudged Jess and they both cheered and waved at me. I was so happy they were there.

"I knew you'd make it!" Jess mouthed.

"Molly!" I heard someone yell from behind.

It was Ed, rushing over to me as quickly as he could without slipping on the tiles. "I *knew* you'd show up. You're going to be amazing."

"Thanks, Ed," I said, turning pink.

And then, without warning, Ed leaned over and kissed me on the cheek.

"Good luck," he said, then turned and walked the other way.

I couldn't believe it. Alice changed the subject quickly, not knowing where to look.

"Err ... OK. Concentrate for a second. This race is exactly what you've done before in practice," she said. "It's four lengths of front crawl. Just focus on yourself, not anybody else. You've got this."

I looked up at her.

"Alice," I said. "Thank you for believing in me when I didn't believe in myself."

She smiled down at me.

"You've got this," she repeated, smiling, and left me standing next to the three girls I was competing against.

That's when I noticed something. All the girls I was swimming against had the same body shape as mine. They didn't look petite and small like Neada, or thin like Chloe and Jess. They were strong, with broad shoulders and legs. We may not have looked like the girls in magazines but we still looked great in our own way.

Looks aside, we were all clearly nervous about the race.

We put our goggles on. I took in a deep breath and looked at the end of the pool ahead of me.

"*You've got this*," I whispered to myself.

I watched the team take their seats on the sidelines. Mr Davidson waved at me to show me he was there. Everyone in the crowd was waiting anxiously for the horn to go off, their excited mumbles echoing around the room.

I glanced up one last time and spotted Nan, Grandad, Neada, Jess and Ed waving at me, their arms a blur with excitement. Their faces were covered in huge grins and they were chanting my name:

"Mol-ly! Mol-ly! Mol-ly!"

If this was what being an Olympic swimmer felt like, this is how I wanted to feel forever.

Three...

Two...

One!

The horn rang and I threw myself head first into the water, pushing my arms and legs forward like I was a motorboat. I didn't look at the girls racing on either side of me. Instead, I just pushed and pushed myself, coming up for air when I needed to.

I swam for Nan and all the times she'd stuck up for me. I swam for Grandad, Alice and Mr Davidson, who believed I was the best swimmer out there. I swam for Ed, who I knew cared about me deeply. And I put all the anger I had towards Mum, Chloe and Tom into driving me forward.

My arms quickly began to ache, but I just didn't stop.

"*Mol-ly! Mol-ly! Mol-ly!*"

Before I knew it, the first lap was done. I took a big kick at the end of the pool and swam back the other way, splashing my legs as hard as I could.

By lap three my legs were aching badly. My arms were heavy and I wanted to stop. But the cheers around me meant I was far from finishing.

"*Come on!*" I thought to myself, coming up for air. "*You never have to swim again after this if you don't want to!*"

I clenched my jaw together in pain. My arms were burning in pain by this point. Just one lap to go, and I'd be finished…

I slammed my hand on the wall in front of me and let out a sigh of relief.

A man yelled my name, and the cheers grew louder and louder. Mr Davidson and Alice rushed over to me, helping me out of the pool and wrapping me in a towel. My arms and legs still ached but the smiles on their faces made it all worthwhile.

"You came second!" Mr Davidson yelled. "You did it! You got a silver medal, Molly!"

20

Nan wouldn't stop crying and saying how proud she was of me. Grandad's face was beaming with a smile I hadn't seen in a long time. Mr Davidson and Alice were hugging each other. Neada, Jess and Ed were jumping around in excitement, cheering my name.

I couldn't believe how much me entering this contest meant to other people. And I couldn't believe I'd almost jeopardised it over what people thought about me, or by worrying about Mum not being there.

She didn't need to be. I had the people I cared

about most around me.

"Come on," Grandad said to Nan, who was blowing her nose. "Let's go and get you a cup of tea."

"See!" Ed said as they walked away, jokingly poking my arm. "I told you you could do it!"

All of a sudden, Neada's face dropped. She pointed behind me and we all turned to look.

It was Chloe, her hair tied back in a loose ponytail and a sad look on her face. She was dressed in a pink tracksuit, but her expression wasn't as bright as the colour she was wearing.

Her mum was standing next to her, a hand on her shoulder and a huge scowl on her face.

"Chloe has a few words she wants to say," she said, and nudged Chloe forward.

There was an awkward silence, with no one knowing where to look. Jess glanced at her feet and Neada folded her arms. Mr Davidson and Alice slowly moved away so they wouldn't interfere.

"I'm so sorry," Chloe blurted out. "I have been the worst friend to you and I am so ashamed of myself."

I couldn't believe it. In all the years I'd known

Chloe, she'd never apologised – not *once*.

I hated Chloe for the horrible things she'd said and done to us all, but I *did* know it would've taken her a lot of guts to say sorry. I noticed Neada's and Jess's crumpled expressions slowly soften.

"Keep going," Chloe's mum said, squeezing her shoulder. She did not look pleased with Chloe at all.

"I've been the worst person in the world to you all and said some dreadful things. I know my dad leaving us doesn't excuse anything, but I don't know what's come over me. This just isn't the person I am."

She turned to Ed.

"I'm so sorry, Ed," she said. He brushed the hair out of his eyes to look at her properly. "I was just really jealous of you and Molly being friends and was worried about you taking Molly away from me." Then she turned to Neada and Jess. "I've been awful to you too. And to Gabby Morris. I'm going to apologise to her properly when I see her."

Her eyes began welling up. She couldn't have been more sorry if she'd tried, and I really didn't want to see her any more upset than she clearly was.

"It's OK," Ed said, his mouth turning into a crooked smile. "I don't want us to fall out."

"Me neither," said Neada.

"Nor me," Jess agreed. "I just want the gang to be back to how it once was."

Chloe looked at me for approval. Yes, she was beautiful. Yes, all the boys fancied her and she had a mum who spoiled her rotten. But I had something she didn't have – a nan and grandad who weren't split down the middle. I was spoiled in other ways. And Chloe would never be strong enough to win a swimming medal like I just had.

"I don't ever, ever, ever want us to fall out again," I said, and all five of us fell into a massive hug, like nothing had ever happened.

"There," Chloe's mum said. "That wasn't difficult, now, was it?"

She wandered off, leaving us still hugging. I knew it would take time, but I was glad our gang could slowly go back to being how we once were.

It was time for me to go home. I'd received my medal and had my photo taken with the other finalists, with my fans (OK – friends and family) gazing adoringly at me. It quite possibly could have been the best day of my life.

I loved the fact that the others were ogling my silver medal. I felt so proud of myself. Ed had done well too, winning himself bronze along with some other people on our team. Out of all the schools competing, our school had won the most medals.

I was just about to say bye to everyone when Chloe suddenly yelled out to someone behind me.

"Oi, you!" she said as the waves in the pool gently whooshed about. "What do you think you're doing here?"

It was Tom Beckett, standing on his own and about to take a bite into a sandwich. His group of loyal Sheep were nowhere to be seen, and his eyes widened at the sight of us.

I felt a lump in my throat and my tummy felt funny. The horror from last Sunday came back into my mind and my legs turned to jelly.

"I heard about what you did to my best friend!" Chloe snapped, and she stormed over to him. Ed followed her, along with Neada and Jess.

Tom wasn't the same cocky, confident boy

without his Sheep with him. All of a sudden he found himself surrounded by a group of people on his own. His eyes had a look of terror in them and he didn't know what to do.

"I ... I..." he muttered, looking at Chloe and then back at me in fear.

"Who do you think you are?" Neada yelled.

"No one gets away with treating my friend like that!" added Jess.

I wasn't sure how they all knew about the chocolate incident but I suppose news travels fast. Needless to say, I was glad they hadn't mentioned it to me.

Tom began stuttering again, taking a few steps back.

"If you think you're going to come anywhere near her or us at St Margaret's, you're wrong," Chloe hissed.

"Yeah," Jess added. "If you mess with one of us, you mess with *all* of us!"

Then, with a giant push, Ed flung out his arms and sent Tom flying into the pool fully clothed.

I burst out laughing and covered my mouth with my hands.

"Now, stay away!" Chloe added, and the three

of them laughed and laughed at Tom flapping around in the water like a fish.

Suddenly the idea of St Margaret's didn't seem scary to me at all. I knew secondary school and life would have its ups and downs, but I wasn't afraid of facing them head-on any more. I didn't need to worry about pleasing other people. With my friends by my side, I knew I'd be fine.

I knew I could handle anything that came my way. And no matter what happened in the future, I knew I'd make a splash.

Acknowledgements

A big thank you must firstly go to all of the girls and women who never give up on their dreams. You inspire us to keep going! This book was inspired by the women whose talents have often been overlooked by the fact they're not societally 'perfect' – the girls who have felt pressured to become somebody else or to look a certain way, as though their appearance is of more importance than what's on the inside. A lot of these pressures start when girls are about to hit puberty, like Molly, and they often think they have to dumb themselves down in order to be accepted. I hope Molly's story shows you that there's nothing better than being yourself and following your heart!

A HUGE thank you to Tom Bonnick and the rest of the Nosy Crow team, whose attention to detail has been second to none.

And finally, a big thank you to my agent, Adam Gauntlett, at PFD, who believed in my writing when nobody else did.